HOW TO FIND
YOUR VISION
AND
GET A LIFE!

*Using a vision and mission
to create a life worth living*

TERRY DREW KARANEN

HOW TO FIND YOUR VISION AND GET A LIFE!
USING A VISION AND MISSION TO CREATE A LIFE WORTH LIVING

by Terry Drew Karanen

Cover photography by Joshua Earle
Cover design by Juan Carlos Negretti Briceño
Author photo by Dennis Martin

Copyright © 2015 by Terry Drew Karanen
First Printing 2015
Printed in the United States of America
Karanen, Terry Drew

How to Find Your Vision and Get a Life! Using a vision and mission help create a life worth living / by Terry Drew Karanen
Develops the process for creating vision and mission statements for individuals, couples and organizations. Includes seventeen self-assessment exercises, appendix with additional suggestions for guidance, and suggested readings.

iUniverse books may be ordered through booksellers or by contacting:

iUniverse
1663 Liberty Drive
Bloomington, IN 47403
www.iuniverse.com
1-800-Authors (1-800-288-4677)

ISBN: 978-1-4917-6947-8 (sc)
ISBN: 978-1-4917-6948-5 (e)

Print information available on the last page.

iUniverse rev. date: 06/08/2015

Praise for

How to Find Your Vision and Get a Life!
Using a vision and mission to create a life worth living

I've dedicated myself to helping people live exceptional lives for more than 30 years, helping thousands of people use results-based strategies to take "quantum leaps" in all areas of life. Terry's new book, *How to Find Your Vision and Get a Life!* provides simple, easy explanations to the challenges of life without the metaphysical psycho-babble often seen in topics like this. Through relating his own life challenges he provides the reader with practical, usable exercises to clarify his/her purpose in life and how to best fulfill that vision and mission – James Mapes, author of *Quantum Leap Thinking: An Owner's Guide to the Mind*

I thoroughly enjoyed reading Terry Drew Karanen's newest book, *How to Find Your Vision and Get a Life! Using a vision and mission to create a life worth living*. So often books in the spirituality or self-help genres end up being more of an edict on what we must do, instead of being the guides they are meant to be. In *Get a Life!* Terry doesn't preach, he shares ideas. His ability to relate both his successes in life as well as his personal demons provide a refreshing atmosphere to promote action and healing for the reader. I was especially impressed with the many exercises he includes to help the reader find their own path and answers. Excellent reading! – Dennis Merritt Jones, author of *Your (Re)Defining Moments: Becoming who you were born to be*

How to Find Your Vision and Get a Life! provides a practical roadmap to a more fulfilled and joyful life. As the author suggests, our true happiness is within reach. It provides insights into the process of discovering our true Divinity through deeper understanding of spiritual principles, practical exercises, and the use of vision and mission processes. The bibliography by itself is one of the best I have seen on the field of life enrichment through spiritual practices. – Rev. J. Robert Gale, Ph.D., Chief Operating Officer (retired), United Church of Religious Science and Dean (retired), Holmes Institute

This inspiring and practical "how-to" book, *How to Find Your Vision and Get a Life!* is clearly and gently written in Terry's authentic and humorous style that engages the reader immediately and leads him or her through sound processes that are expertly designed to open to a life of new possibilities. He creates and sustains a feeling that one is in attendance at a lively seminar in which the participant feels safe, supported, and awakened to a greater vision and mission for life. As he presents excellent examples and guides the reader through practical exercises, it is obvious that he has effectively used these processes himself, as the teacher cannot take the student to a place that he has not also traveled. – Maxine Kaye, author of *Alive and Ageless: How to Feel Alive and Live Fully Every Day of Your Life*

Terry Drew Karanen describes bliss as having a love affair with life. To nurture and sustain such a love requires a clear vision and a lifestyle commitment. Karanen's latest book, *How to Find Your Vision and Get a Life!* is the perfect helpmate in deepening your bliss commitment and learning to trust your heart. Wonderfully written and clearly detailed, this book will help you do exactly that! – David Ault, author of *The Grass Is Greener Right Here*

After 80 years of living, with challenges, ups and downs, fears, and accomplishments, I am again ready for my next phase or project life has for me. With the help and guidance of Terry Drew Karanen's book, *Get a Life!* and following his suggested exercises, I am ready to decide what that will be. – Marilyn Leo, author of *Chronicles of Religious Science*

I know of Terry's work as a minister and counselor, but *How to Find Your Vision and Get a Life!* was my first experience of Terry as an author. As a movie/drama critic, I know my readers expect me to dissect the media I review with a critical eye. I take my job very seriously because I know what I write often determines whether my readers see a film or decide to skip it. It's always a pleasure to be able to acknowledge the work of an artist as being worthwhile and I'm proud to be able to do that for Terry's latest book. If *How to Find Your Vision and Get a Life!* was a film, it would be a solid 10 on the Granger Movie Gauge of 1 to 10! – Susan Granger, SSG Syndicate, on-air television and radio commentator and entertainment critic

Terry is clearly passionate about bliss, and clearly excited about helping other people discover their own bliss. In *How to Find Your Vision and Get a Life!* he lays out his process for you to discover your vision and mission, essential elements, he tells us, for creating a life that is worth living. The exercises are practical and the stories are personal and through the words the reader gets a sense of how enthusiastic Terry is about sharing what has worked so well in his life. – Edward Viljoen, author of *The Power of Meditation*

Books and Booklets by Terry Drew Karanen

Empowerment
How to Find Your Vision and Get a Life! Using a vision and mission to create a life worth living
Freedom to Live! Enjoying ease in four areas of life)
It's Safe for Me to Be …
Meditations for Life! — The Wisdom of Women
Meditations for Life! (Originally published as *Treatments for Life!*)

Church Organization & Management

Beginning Your Own Work

Humor
The Res Book

Short Stories
The Beverage Service

Dedication

This book is dedicated to my niece, Kalee Scolatti, who lived her vision every day by simply being the amazing woman and mother she was. You made your uncle Frank and me very proud.

Chapter One

You Can Have a Life Worth Living

You probably picked up this book because there is something you would like to be doing with your life or your career that you are currently not doing.

You most likely have all kinds of reasons why you cannot begin doing the very thing you would really like to do. You may have accumulated dramatic examples to justify those reasons to yourself and others why this is so. You may even have well-crafted stories you have told yourself and anyone who will listen that supports your beliefs.

You may have surrounded yourself with family and friends who are more than willing to agree with you. They are probably not doing what they want to be doing either. This situation has the effect of making everyone concerned feel very comfortable, because even though no one is really happy at least everyone has someone with whom to be miserable!

Bars and cocktail lounges are filled with people at "Happy Hour" far busier complaining about their jobs than they were at working at those occupations just a few hours before. Commiserating together, along with the relaxing effect of a few adult beverages, allows people to believe that even though their lives are not the way they think they should be, or dream they could be, at least there are others as bad off, or perhaps even worse off than they are.

It is my belief, completely unproven to my knowledge by any scientific studies, that reality TV shows exist for one of two reasons: To watch people live lives we have convinced ourselves are out of our reach, thereby shoring up any doubt that we can have what we want; or, to insure that regardless how bad our lives may look at times, there are people out there that are somehow amazingly even more screwed up than we thought were on our very worst day. The latter, of course, encourages us to be satisfied with, if not proud of, the status quo since it is light years ahead of the people we are watching.

There is a pervasive belief among what I believe to be the majority of people that the past has a tremendous influence on the present and the future. As a licensed social worker and counselor I accept that the past can affect us, but not in the way most people believe. A common belief is that if circumstances have occurred in a particular and consistent way over the course of time, then it must stand to reason that such circumstances will continue to evolve in the same manner. This is not true.

Universal laws or principles govern our lives. This is a timeless metaphysical truth. We do not get to vote on this. It is not something about which to argue any more than changing the law of gravity is up for discussion. What is important to recognize is that both physical and metaphysical laws affect us whether or not we profess our belief in them. But, the more we know about how these laws work the more we are going to be able to enjoy the life we want.

These laws are immutable, which means that they are not subject to change, nor are they susceptible to any outside influence. Unlike human authority figures, the laws of the universe cannot be bought, bribed or coerced into changing. The past we have experienced is a result of where we were in consciousness at that time. The difference is that where we were does not have to affect where we are or where we want to be unless we choose to allow it to do so.

The laws are totally impartial. The laws work the same for each of us, regardless of race, ethnic background, religion, gender or sexual orientation. They respond to our thoughts in a unique and consistent manner. The laws respond to our core beliefs, the paradigms we find guiding our life. This means that your present thought is the only important one. All other thoughts are in the past, which you can do nothing, or in the future that has yet to arrive.

You can start having the life you want today by first being willing to believe it is possible. Changing your thinking in the present begins to transform old beliefs, which may no longer serve you, into a new and exciting matrix for your present and future. That is the beginning of a new path toward the realization and fulfillment of your life purpose. That is the beginning of a new path to happiness.

Precedent does not bind universal law. Just because something has always been our experience in the past does not mean it has to continue to be our experience now or in the future. We do not have to keep going from one lousy job to another or from one unsatisfactory relationship to another. One of my teachers once said:

The world knows you in terms of your history, but the universe knows you in terms of how you are knowing yourself at this present moment.

Most of us are far too concerned with what the world *thinks* of us instead of what the universe *knows* about us. Spirit knows that we are magnificent, unique and abundantly supplied in all we require. Scripture says that before we even ask for what we want the Father has anticipated our need (Matthew 6:8). The reason it looks as if God knows before we do is that God is responding to our inner consciousness, the subconscious. This may or may not be what we are *saying* we want. It is most assuredly what we *believe* in our hearts that we deserve, even if it is destructive.

Let me pause in our discussion for a small sidebar on a big issue to many people: "God." I have no idea what your spiritual or religious beliefs are, or if you have any at all. I personally believe in an intelligence that is greater than we are, but that same consciousness lives in, through and as us in unique ways.

This power many people call God. I also see it as Spirit, divine love, universal consciousness, Goddess, energy and many other terms. If one word doesn't work for you, substitute one that does. If you are atheist or agnostic, replace God in this book with science, energy or your own consciousness. As you may have already figured out, I believe that whatever we accomplish we do from our center, our inner being, or our own volition.

In the universal scheme of things there is only the *now*. We can change our lives today; the only thing standing in the way is the old belief that it is impossible to change our situation. If we are open to being guided by Spirit – which to me amounts to following our intuition – our lives can be transformed. All spiritual masters teach us about intuition. It is what some call "the still small voice." By this they mean the quiet, intuitive nature of Spirit, whispering softly to us, privately and uniquely about how best to proceed on our individual paths. In this book you will learn how to hear and trust that voice without fear that the mental health community will brand you as psychotic.

There is another voice inside most of us. It is the voice of our critic. It does not whisper; it usually screams at the top of its lungs! It is what some call the *ego mind* and others refer to as the *logical mind*. It certainly plays an important role in our lives, but it wants nothing to do with a life based on intuition. It wants provable facts backed up with experience.

Most of the experience it recalls to us are the experiences of failure, disappointment and heartache. It is the first voice we hear after a relationship has ended and we are finally willing to risk again. It is the voice that becomes indignant at any thought of leaving a job we hate because we are vested in a retirement plan. It is the voice that says a sore throat has to be the beginning of a two-week bout with the flu. It is not our enemy. It is only doing the best it can to help us avoid further hurt and pain. The information it has is biased and that is the danger. It says, "Don't risk," yet risk is required if we are to grow.

Consider a toddler learning to walk. Her first steps without the help of someone else or lacking the security of leaning on the coffee table are apt to be somewhat shaky at best. Her mother or father might rejoice at just one step, even if that's followed by a resounding fall to the floor. The toddler does not stop. Yes, she fell, and she gets up and tries again to walk. Eventually she will walk in a steady manner and be able to run, jump and leap at will. It takes courage to keep trying and it takes practice to perfect this task.

How can a child have such courage? What is the driving force behind such determination? It may look like courage to us because we are quick to think of what might happen should she fall into the corner of the coffee table. We might even be reminded of falling down and hurting ourselves when we were children. The toddler has no such history. She has no point of reference to create a fear to overcome. She simply knows what she wants. That is the driving force. She is determined to move about. It is the sole focus of her life at that given moment. That type of belief in success and that example of determination to reach our goal is the same factor that will allow us to accomplish whatever we set out to do.

We are not toddlers. We have histories and stories. Our inner critic is well-versed in the abundance of facts about past failures, dangers, potential pitfalls and excuses. As if all that were not enough, it can sometimes appear that our inner critic is supported by a cast of thousands. You might already know who, in your own life, voices the concerns of your inner critic.

As you read through this book your inner critic will surface. When it does, stop to thank it for its concern, and then let it know that you are under new management. You are going to try something new and that it will turn out just fine. Make sure it understands that you are aware of the potential risks and that you feel the probability of success is worth it.

It is strongly suggested that you share your new thoughts and plans discreetly. This minimizes criticism from other people. Share only with people whom you know will support you in being the magnificent creature you are. If you know your step-father is going to put down anything new you try to do, then do not set yourself up to lose by sharing your precious vision and dreams with such a person.

You may remember hearing someone quote the words of Jesus in the Gospel about casting pearls before swine (Matthew 7:6). This is what the Great Teacher was showing his disciples. We do not judge the swine. Pigs are pigs and that works just fine in the universal scheme of life. Pigs just have no use for pearls. We do. Pearls are expensive, beautiful and have no place in the hog trough. There's nothing wrong with the hog trough – it's just not for pearls. Got it? Good, because now you won't throw any of your own pearls of wisdom in that direction.

We are our own worst critics, but we can also be our own best cheerleaders. There is only one person responsible when it comes down to who is stopping you from having your life be the way you want it: You. All that you've read up to this point is the preparation you need as you to embark on a journey that may take you into areas you have not yet explored in your life and consciousness. You may also encounter areas that you think you have already handled. This thinking is correct. Now you are ready to peel off another layer, go a little deeper, heal a little more and grow closer toward the life you know you want.

Reading this far and dealing with the thoughts in your own consciousness that have already surfaced has taken a great deal of courage. Acknowledge yourself for this! You are one of a growing number of people on this planet willing to take responsibility for their life. That takes far more courage than staying stuck and complaining about what our parents did or did not do, what the government should do or how our health inhibits us from living the life we want.

You are pretty magnificent to do this for yourself. The exercises and instruction in this book will empower you to:

Discover your keys to happiness;

Create a vision statement to guide your life; and,

Write a mission statement to carry out your vision.

You will begin to transform your life into something awesome, perhaps in a way you never dreamed possible. Doing so will also move our planet to another level of consciousness, peace, harmony, joy, love and full self-expression.

In the next five chapters I intend to share with you the "Five P's" of having a life worth living:

Possibility

Power

Passion

Practice

Purpose

These five individual components along with developing clear intention in your life will lead you to creating your own vision and missions statements. They will provide a firm foundation upon which to create a life truly worth living.

Chapter Two

Possibility

Possibility is where we shall begin. It's fairly easy to say we're happy about something. But ask yourself this: What emotions get stirred up inside you that bring that happiness to the highest level?

The answer to that question will be individual and unique. The highest level of happiness often includes more than one emotion and can include several feelings. A word used for such happiness is sometimes referred to as "bliss," but that term can be confusing because of perceived ideas we may have about it.

First we must determine what bliss is to us individually. This is necessary if we intend to consider the possibility of having a life of happy, blissful experiences. What is bliss to you? Stop for a moment right now. Close your eyes and ponder that question for a moment. Get a clear idea of what bliss feels like to you. Then continue reading.

Here are some of the thoughts that have been suggested from people I've interviewed:

Love

Dirty

Lust

Happiness

Ecstasy

Ignorance is bliss

Friends

Satisfaction

Fulfillment

Play

Physical Well-Being

Peace

Joy

Evil

Freedom

That is quite a wide range of opinions. Some of the beliefs people often hold about is that it's not attainable in the modern world, not a sustainable experience, or not a practical state-of-mind. A blissful person is frequently depicted as either dead, an idiot who does not understand the seriousness of life, or some kind of religious fanatic who is so spiritually high they are of no earthly good. I believe we can, to the best of our ability, live with a blissful attitude about each and every minute of each and every day. Who decides what "best" is? I do in my life; you do in your life. Some days I do pretty well, other days are more of a challenge.

If someone suggests there just might be a better way to live, we might find a red flag being waved frantically. The ego is the one holding that flag with tenacity. The ego is no fan of change. Even if the change will better the situation our ego usually has to be convinced. It is as if our ego is saying, "I didn't think of that possibility or solution so it must not be valid." Another favorite of the ego is, "That's too easy. It cannot be that easy." One remark I sometimes hear from a student is, "Oh, so because you believe in living a blissful life I suppose your life is always perfect, right?"

The Perfect Life

I've been asked, "So is *your* life perfect?" The answer is "yes," which generally annoys the one asking that question in the sarcastic manner in which it is posed. My answer is coming from the metaphysical principles upon which I base and live my life. From that vantage point everything is perfect because my life is responding in the manner that corresponds exactly to the way I have put universal laws into motion.

Those laws have responded to my subconscious thought and or conscious desire and thereby produced my belief "perfectly." The English word "perfect" comes from the Latin *perfectus*, past participle of *perficere*, meaning to finish, or *per* + *facere*, to be done (The New Century Dictionary, 1952).

If something is perfect then it just means it works the way it was intended. The catch is that our conscious intention is often superseded by our subconscious belief system. A perfect life does not mean a life without problems; it is a life that works. Most of my life works for me most of the time. When I don't feel I'm getting the results I want, I change my thinking and produce a different outcome.

I'd say that's perfect. I used to feel if my plans worked the way I thought they would, *then* it was perfect. If events were different than I expected, I would be disappointed. I'm still disappointed at times, but I also have a lot less attachment to the outcome in the first place. Why? Because I'm willing to take responsibility for my life.

Someone else may look at the way I live and find it most unappealing. To them my life is far from perfect. I've found that the majority of people who find fault with my life and my multiple careers are usually unhappy with their own life and careers. Since I'm having a pretty fabulous time with my life I pay little attention to them most of the time. If people are criticizing and questioning you, pay no attention to them as well, unless you know deep within yourself that there is a grain of truth what they are saying.

Perfection is a relative concept. How your life is judged is all in the perspective of the individual. I'm sure you have no problem understanding that! The teacher in me, however, feels the need to give you an example for added clarity, so here is an example: A tuxedo is *perfect* for attending a formal function. It is *not so perfect* for doing the gardening. Just because we do not use a tux to do the gardening doesn't mean it is not perfect for the opera. Does that put the word *perfect* into a slightly different light for you?

Another reason why I determine my life to be perfect is because of the way I remember my life before I found the principles I now live by. In the early 1980s I lived daily with horrible pain. The medical profession told me there was nothing that could be done since the pain was caused by rheumatoid arthritis and deemed incurable. At first I believed them. I thought I would live a life of agony until I died. Shortly after receiving the "verdict" of my doctor I got sick and tired of being sick and tired. I had had enough of the pain.

Through sheer determination of mind and a radical change in diet, I removed the so-called incurable disease from my body – a fact that was later recorded by medical doctors and a battery of tests. Not long after that, I went through a divorce and found myself alone in the world. The hopelessness and loneliness I felt was an even bigger problem than the one I had recently overcome. I chose to deal with this situation through over-working, over-drinking, over-drugging, over-sexing and over-spending myself into a man who one day could not even get out of bed. I was barely eating. I had bills that were double my small salary. I felt like no one cared whether I lived or died – including God.

It was then that I stumbled into my first real experience of understanding metaphysical principles. A friend took me to a small church that was based on the philosophy of a man named Ernest Holmes. He had developed a method of blending science, philosophy, religion and spirituality. I was astounded and my close friends will tell you that seldom happens.

Those principles and the love of others in the congregation helped me on the road to recovery from near suicide. I learned about possibility thinking in the face of a no-win situation. I learned about thinking positively when I only saw a negative outcome. It wasn't that I had to learn some new teaching or dogma. I learned that I needed to radically overhaul my belief systems. I had to learn how to think in a new way.

Today my life is very, very different. I maintain close relationships with my biological family. I surround myself with a loving, supportive, extended and growing family of choice. I have healed wounds I suffered and caused in many past personal relationships. I continue the healing process in yet other situations. I pay my bills. I support myself while I help others to see possibilities when their situations look impossible. My body is healthy and strong.

Are there other things I want? Do I have "bad hair days?" Am I able to see where I can improve? Sure. And, yes, I still say my life is perfect.

Living in Bliss

I can also say that I experience bliss in my life on a daily basis. The kind of bliss I am speaking about is not the kind of bliss we sometimes see on TV or in a movie. You know what I mean. It's the story where the person's body appears to be here on this plane while his consciousness is somewhere else. Bliss does not have to mean that we are oblivious to what is going on around us; that we forget to eat, or sleep, or stop at red lights or feed the cat.

It does mean a kind of love affair with life. It can appear in the form of awe when we see a sunrise or the multitude of stars on a clear night. It can be a smile of satisfaction when something we have planned seems to fall into place effortlessly. Part of the bliss I experience is going to bed almost every night with a feeling of accomplishment, fulfillment and satisfaction.

Playing With Possibility

Most of us are far too concerned with being busy. We see endless possibilities before us because so much has become available to us in the last century. We can be tempted to desire everything at once. Instead of enjoying the freedom produced by labor-saving devices we can easily become a slave to them. We need to take more time, even plan more time, to play. It is through play that Spirit can begin to open our hearts and minds to the many possibilities before us that will simplify, not complicate, our lives. Our creative, intuitive mind is accessed and utilized to its full potential through play.

In her classic book, *The Artist's Way*, Julia Cameron (1992) suggests we take what she calls an "artist's date" once a week, and an "artist's day" periodically. The artist's date is a two- or three-hour period of time, uninterrupted and alone for us to enjoy some leisure or playful activity. The artist's day is the same, only a *full day* of leisure and play…alone… without friends…without family… and without your mobile phone, tablet or anything else electronic.

It is during these play periods that our creativity will blossom. Ideas will come to us. New opportunities will present themselves. Does it work? From personal experience I can tell you it does. Will it work for you? Like everything else in life, it will work for you if you expect it to work for you. Your ego will tell you it's stupid, illogical and counterproductive to all the work you need to do. But it's your ego that may have stopped you from living life to the fullest, so I would not heed its call to caution in this particular case. Go out and play. Find out for yourself.

Your Belief System

In chapter one I referred to the core beliefs we hold about life. This can also be called our *belief system*. You can do anything with a belief system that supports your idea of what you want your life to be. Begin to declare that which you wish to become now, even if your life is not reflecting such beliefs. This type of reprogramming of our subconscious has been called *fake it until you make it.* It is acting as if what you want your life to be is already a reality. The effectiveness of this process has been documented since the early 1960s when biofeedback became popular.

It is not my purpose to take the time and space necessary to discuss this process in depth. If this is a totally new concept to you, I recommend you do some additional research and self-study. At the back of this book there is a list of recommended readings. Take a moment to become still and then turn to that section. Allow your eyes to scan over the list. You will settle on one or two as if they have jumped off the page at you. Run, do not walk, to your local bookstore, library or web browser and obtain the ones to which you are drawn.

As you begin to reprogram your belief system there will be thoughts of disbelief that will come up. Years ago I attended a prosperity class. The instructor suggested using what she called the *cancel method*. If a negative or unproductive thought pops up, she taught us to say "CANCEL" out loud, and then follow that statement with another more positive thought in line with the new belief system. By doing this you are not only thinking about obliterating the old paradigm, you are verbalizing it and you are hearing it being said in your own voice.

The more senses we can bring into this process, the better. If you are around other people this might prove interesting, but at least you will be having fun with the process. I once heard that one definition of the word *interesting* translates as, "God, I hope I live through this!" Trust me. You will live through a few somewhat dismayed stares or questioning glances. Find solace in the fact that you will be great material for their dinner discussion that evening.

Make it a fun exercise and enjoy yourself. Personally, I enjoy doing things that allow me to walk out of a store with a smile on my face while leaving everyone still standing in line with their mouths open. Call it a Cosmic Giggle.

What is Your Intention?

One of the main reasons I teach the value of vision and mission statements through this book, in seminars and in private consultation is to assist more people to find their life purpose and eventually have a career that promotes their vision. At this point though, get the idea of *job* out of the joy of finding your happiness. Too many people get involved in discovering their life purpose and then stop short of living it because they cannot figure out how to make money doing it. Making money is not the intention, although prosperity will begin to flow with ease when you discover your true desire for life and begin to live it.

At this point, and in our lives in general, our intention should be to enjoy ourselves, be fulfilled and help others in the process. Many people are perfectly happy doing a job which pays the bills and leaves a little left over for recreation, if that job allows them the time to pursue what they really love. Doing what they love usually includes others. Even if it does not include others directly, the joy they experience while doing what they love to do overflows into the rest of their lives, thereby helping others.

Think of what you do that pays you money as your "job" and what you do as your living your life purpose as your "work," meaning the work you are here to do on planet earth at this point in the space-time continuum. Maybe they will be one and the same. Maybe not. The idea is that both will be enjoyable.

My first year of being the pastor of a church is an example of this. Shortly after completing my ministerial training my partner at the time and I (along with our two cats) moved across the country from Glendale, California to Pittsburgh, Pennsylvania to start my ministry. I chose to build a church from scratch, not the building, but the ministry within the structure of a church community.

Besides the Sunday services and programs, there were classes to develop and teach, music preparation, counseling sessions, ceremonies, pastoral care for the growing congregation and community, and the legal paperwork required to begin any business. I worked about 40 hours plus per week doing all the tasks a founding minister does when one is starting and maintaining a church.

I also held down a full-time position as a legal secretary. My secretarial responsibilities included interacting with two or more attorneys on a daily basis, creating and revising union contracts, negotiating labor disputes and handling various human resource issues.

For over a year I was working nearly 80 hours per week. I do remember on more than one occasion falling asleep at the computer that sat on a cardboard box on the floor of the room that eventually became my home office. The computer sat on a cardboard box because when we made our move we decided not to move any furniture across country. We ended up sleeping on the floor for six months through the coldest and most severe winter Pittsburgh had seen in about a hundred years. It was rough at times.

What kept me going was that after all those years of training, all the classes, all the critiques and all the testing, *I was finally doing ministry!* No, I did not want to continue doing secretarial work, but working at that job paid the rent on the apartment, gave me the money to rent space to have a Sunday morning and Wednesday evening service, and bought food. It allowed me to do something to which I was totally committed: Serving others as a minister.

Changing Your Thinking – Change Your Job!

If the job you are currently in does not fit your picture perhaps you could begin changing your belief system about it. I sure had to when my desk was covered with contract revisions instead of my Sunday talk outline. The universe is adamant about many things. Here is one of those things: Whatever you give your attention to increases. If what you are doing is complaining about your job (or anything else for that matter), the complaining can only make a bad situation worse. Begin to change your belief system about the job by changing your attitude immediately.

Find the benefit – *any* benefit – to working where you are right now. I recognized what wonderful people the attorneys I worked with were, the benefits of being there, and the energy of being in that particular office. When I did that my situation shifted dramatically. The same can happen for you *if* you are willing to commit to doing so.

I once heard it said that the words *work* and *worship* come from the same root word. Our work can be worship of God or of whatever Higher Power you conceive. Would you be willing to see your job as a sacred act? Stop laughing hysterically for a minute and consider that question. It may seem impossible at first, but what fun to do that at least for a week! Please note that I said *do it* not *try it*. In the words of the wise Yoda from *Star Wars: The Empire Strikes Back* when he was mentoring young Luke Skywalker:

Try not. Do, or do not. There is no try.

We can have fun and worship at the same time. The universe is a place of joy, merriment and fun! I stay as far as possible away from churches and spiritual groups who think God is all about being serious. Jesus and the original twelve apostles all enjoyed having a good time. Gandhi enjoyed life and knew the value of laughter. Buddha and the bodhisattvas were known for playing tricks on unsuspecting disciples. If you read some of the accounts of the lives and experiences of the saints they might even be described as impish!

My friend and former instructor, Dr. Arleen Bump, is the spiritual leader of a successful church. She flatly states that if she cannot have a good time doing what she is doing then she is simply not interested. She is out of there…period. You have Jesus and the other Masters, most of the apostles, Dr. Arleen and me telling you it is okay to enjoy life. If that's not enough, the Bible is full of passages where God tells you to be happy. Do it!

I believe you *can* have a good time *most* of the time. Nothing except the universal principles I'm discussing are going to be the same 100 percent of the time, but you can have a good time for the majority of each day. There is a price to pay. You knew there was a catch, right? That old saying that you do not get something for nothing applies here. You have to give up something, probably something you are holding onto tenaciously.

I do not mean your current job, or a relationship, or any other responsibilities you might have. I mean giving up something that might be part of the foundation of your life. I mean giving up something that may have stopped you for years. How about giving up the idea that you cannot have the life you want? How about giving up a belief in lack and limitation? How about giving up the idea that you are not good enough?

17

Take time to meditate on what you believe about life, career, relationships, health and money. See if you can identify any beliefs that no longer serve you. Be willing to question what you believe deep down inside your private thoughts. Any Truth can stand up to questioning. False beliefs, like false teachings and teachers, will wither away. If some of your beliefs are shaky, find out why. Their foundations just might be built on the shifting, sandy soil of misguided, false belief, not rock-solid truth.

The Way, The Right Way or Your Way?

So many people miss out on the success of living the life they were meant to live because they try to live the way someone else is living. Your best friend's life might be working for them, but you are not that person. We need to develop our own way of doing things. After three years of doing ministry the way I had been taught in school I realized I was not happy. It was a difficult puzzle. I had all the right pieces of my vision. I was living a happy life for the most part. I had loving friends in my life. I was happy with myself. My bills were paid. I had a nice home. I was even able to afford comfortable vacations. But something was wrong.

I was very busy doing ministry the way I was taught, following the rules and making sure all my "t's" were crossed and my "i's" were dotted. The problem was that I was too busy doing church to do ministry. I decided to resign from the church so the congregation could secure a new pastor whose vision was closer to theirs in creating a congregation. I was then free to pursue my ministry in a more free-form manner, devoid of rules and regulations, as well as organizational support. It was then that I began to discover my purpose, to truly live my vision.

I discovered a great lack of support for my new independent ministry from former ministerial colleagues, no doubt placed there to perfectly mirror my own self-doubts. As I became clearer on what I wanted my ministry to look like, the doubters fled in droves. They were replaced with new, exciting and vibrant colleagues, ones living their own vision. Some of those ministers are doing that within the traditional structure of church or center. Others are not.

The point here is not that one way of doing ministry is better than another. The point is that as a minister I had to discover which way worked for me in my service to others. If the minister is not being served, he or she will not be able to effectively serve others…at least not for very long, and most certainly not very well.

Before you think this is sounding too religious, please understand that having a ministry has little to do with religion or a church. Your life purpose is *your ministry*. Each of us has a wonderful, unique gift to give to the planet. It is what excites you the most. It is what you need to do. And *you* are the only person on the planet that can do whatever it is that you do precisely the way you do it. To live your life purpose you have to be willing to give that gift and give it in a way that perfectly reflects the essence of who you are.

Exercise #1 - Finding Out What Excites Us!

What is it that really excites you? Something may or may not be coming to mind for you. In either case, here is an exercise to reveal a little more about what you really want to do with your life. As you do the exercise, remember to keep *job* and *making money* out of the process. Go with your first thoughts, no matter how outrageous or outlandish. It is those off-the-wall thoughts we seldom entertain that hold so many precious clues about our happiness.

List 6-10 times in your life when you felt completely fulfilled in the moment.

Look for a commonality in those moments (Example: I found out I loved accomplishing goals. There were two basic problems with this feeling of fulfillment. First, although I was great at reaching goals, I seldom finished the entire project. I would reach the goal and then wander off. Second, if I did complete what I started I almost never took time to recognize my accomplishment. I was too busy looking for the next mountain to climb to stop and celebrate anything.)

When you have found the commonality ask yourself, "Is that the way I want my life to be?" If the answer is "yes", project that kind of energy in everything you do. If the answer is "no", begin to meditate and ponder how you might change your experience.

Continue to work on this list.

I have always wanted to be of service to others. That has not always meant having one particular job. I used to envy people who were focused on just one career. I found myself wishing I had the drive to have wanted to become an Olympic ice skater, a professional dancer, a physician or an attorney. I went to elementary school with other children who had that kind of drive and some of them are doing today exactly what they said they would be doing.

Eventually I came to realize that I'd always wanted to do ministry. I have ministered to thousands of people since I joined the workforce through a variety of jobs and careers. Most of the time I was oblivious to what I was doing for others because it did not *look* like traditional ministry.

Living your life purpose is not only personally rewarding but also assists the planet. People are waiting for you to become even more magnificent than you can imagine right now! By discovering and living your life purpose, you will have to widen the way you view yourself. That means you may have to get the idea of a minister, pastor or priest out of your head when you hear the word *ministry*. Remove the concept of *ministry* from any association with religion or a church. Instead, when you read or hear ministry think of it as *life's work*. This will enable you to be willing to entertain a few new possibilities, ones that may seem fantastic to you.

Exercise #2 - What Do I Want To Be When I Grow Up?

Remember the old question of "What do you want to be when you grow up?" Have you figured out the answer yet? I'm not talking about what you've decided to do for a job or career at this point, particularly if that job or career is feeling less than satisfying. You may or may not have any idea what you really want to do with your life. The following exercise will give you a glimpse of some desires that may be hidden or forgotten. Complete Exercise #2 by answering both questions with a *very* open mind. It is important to do so because in Exercise #3 you will be asked to push yourself even further.

Imagine you are in a huge mall. What kind of store are you in?

Imagine you are in the library. In which section would we find you? To what kind of books are you drawn?

Where you found yourself in the mall or in the library will give you a clue about what really interests you in life. It may indicate what you think of as true happiness. Take a look at the qualities or activities surrounding the store or the section of the library in which you found yourself. Do you have those qualities or activities in your life now? Why or why not? If not, would you be willing to open up to ways in which you could include more of your interests in your daily life?

Exercise #3 - On My Way to Happiness!

Did the previous two exercises push any of your buttons or wake up your ego mind? I promised you in the third exercise you would be asked to push yourself further – and you will. Trust me, it will also be fun. This is *not* a test! The next exercise will ask you to stretch. It will present you with a concept you may find impossible to believe. It may confirm what you have known all along. Take a moment to quiet your mind, be willing to entertain new ideas and then follow the instructions.

Set a timer for three minutes and write down as many things as you can that you like to do. Once again, dismiss any thoughts about these activities being practical, financially viable and feasible, or for which you have the free time. Be free to explore the possibilities.

Pick your top ten favorite activities out of the list.

Now pick your top three choices of those ten activities.

Finally, pick the most desirable activity of the three.

Could that be your career?

If you say "No!" immediately you have slammed the door shut on a universe of possibilities. Yes, it may look completely impossible. Yes, it may sound frivolous. In fact, it may even look illegal.

I remember a perfectly well-adjusted woman whose final choice was sex. She already thought she knew what *that* career was called! In discussing the situation with her I mentioned the possibility of becoming a certified sex therapist. Her initial reaction included a fair amount of blushing along with a few snickers from various parts of the room. "What would people think?!? My mother would just die!"

Later, privately and very quietly, she asked me, somewhat excitedly, "Do you really think I could?" I think you can do anything if you really want to. I do not know whatever became of her, but I do know that for a brief moment that woman opened her consciousness to a new idea and a new possibility. That is all that the universe needs to put into motion all the power necessary to make manifest your intention.

It Is Up to You!

If you are experiencing adverse reactions to these exercises take comfort in knowing that in some way they are your friends. They are taking you in the right direction. They are bringing up the blockages of which you might already be aware or some old ones you may have buried. Before you continue with the next chapter, take some time to digest what you have discovered about yourself thus far.

Are you willing to let go and allow Divine Intelligence to unfold the limitless possibilities before you? The universe awaits your command, but it can only do for you what it can do through you. It cannot provide avenues of growth if in the deepest recesses of your mind you are saying, "No. I cannot grow there yet."

A good reporter covers the five "w's": *who, what, where, when* and *why*, plus *how*. The *how* is perhaps the single, largest contributing factor to our conscious or subconscious reluctance to grow. We do not always get to know *how*. Personally, I find this annoying. I am very analytical and want all the details. But, the *how* is not our job. Our job is to know *what*. The *how* will present itself if we have cleared the way in our consciousness. We must be open to following through when the path is obvious and the time is right. The *how* begins to unfold with ease allowing possibilities to become realities. The way to do that is to recognize our *Power*.

Chapter Three

Power

Our dreams are like tiny seeds. Many seeds are small and easily lost, misplaced or even crushed. There are a fair number of seeds that are nothing like the avocado seed, which takes up nearly half of the fruit. The avocado seed-sized dreams are usually ones that come out of a group consciousness. That group energy can allow the dream to grow more quickly than our own personal dreams. In turn, it is those larger dreams that may show progress more quickly than our small and seemingly less significant personal projects.

The size of the seed we physically plant is irrelevant to how we proceed with what we intend to do for it. We carefully select the seed we want. We prepare the soil and then plant the seed. Additional nutrients are added as well as ample water. We nurture the little plant as it continues to mature. As it grows we gently pull out any weeds that may take root near our precious seedling. Eventually we reap the benefits of our labor as the plant produces flowers or food.

How Seeds Are Like Our Dreams

Our dreams, large or small, are just like the seeds. These seeds, regardless of size, contain within them the potential of the plant. An actual plant has within it the natural ability to produce the flower or the food. Within the dream is the potential for the complete development of the dream's fulfillment. This is a crucial but usually difficult concept for most of us. Our egos want to figure out the whole game plan. We are programmed by culture to see ourselves in control. We really are in one sense, though it may appear to be just the opposite.

Are You Waiting For Your Dream To Come True?

Your dream is waiting for you to come true, not the other way around. Because this is the truth about dreams it may sound like they are some kind of cosmic force, some pre-destined life course that we have to follow. It may seem like the dream is the one in control instead of you. The key here is to understand who put the dream in motion in the first place: You did.

When you speak your word or feel your feelings with power, universal intelligence finds an opportunity in which to do its work. With that opening, no matter how small, Spirit begins to work for you by working through you. That is why it is so important for us to concentrate our energies on *what* we want, letting the universe take care of the *how*.

This process does not for one moment imply a sense of "wait and see" for us. We do not decide we want a new relationship and then sit in front of the TV waiting for him or her to come knocking at our door. We get busy cleaning up our home to be inviting. We take care of ourselves to make sure our body, our clothes and our life is welcoming to that new person. If we stay busy being about our business then Spirit can begin its work on fulfilling our desire. My experience is that God always has a bigger idea of what is possible for me.

My favorite illustration of this comes from my late friend, Don Stepp, who was an artist. One afternoon, a small group of us were sitting around a picnic table at the Asilomar Conference Center in Monterey, California, discussing philosophical points of view. Several of us were in the last stages of our ministerial training – eager to "get there" – and equally impatient to share our "wisdom." At some point we "spiritual masters" all took a breath, giving Don a chance to quickly take center stage with authority and leadership, and with not just a little smile on his face.

Don said that our prayers are like that of a painter asking God to paint a picture for him. It is as if the painter sketches the outline on the canvas and then hands the canvas to God to paint. The problem, according to Don, was that we fail to start out with a big enough canvas. We also expect a masterpiece from God without giving God enough brushes and only a few colors. It was a priceless moment in humility for me.

Sound familiar? It does to me, especially when I think of the requests for relationships I hear from people. The conversation starts off fairly well; they want a relationship. But then the trouble starts! He has to be 31-37 years old; no older, no younger. She has to be blond; a brunette will not fill the order. He has to have a hairy chest. She must like traveling. He cannot have a cat. Blaah, blaah, blaah. It goes on and on and on.

I know of one gay man who was truly open to his perfect relationship. His prayer was for his perfect mate, regardless of age, appearance, economic status or *sex*. I asked him if he really meant that he would marry a woman. I found his words most insightful. Although he admitted he did not picture himself marrying a woman, he also wanted to make sure that all possibilities were open. Then he said that *God wasn't stupid and he had no concern that the universe was going to play some cruel trick on him or some unsuspecting woman.*

One of my dearest friends and teachers, the late Reverend Helen Street, used to say that we are dealing with divine intelligence, not "Big Dummy In The Sky!" The man I mentioned in the preceding paragraph did shortly thereafter begin a relationship with another man and no woman was involved. But who really knows? Perhaps he might have found a woman who was interested in him, they may have dated, he may have told her he was gay, and her deep love for him and his best interests could have led her to introduce him to her gay brother or a friend. Sound far-fetched?

Not necessarily. Our good frequently comes in steps or stages. Going one place leads us to another place, and perhaps another, and still yet, one or more places after that. At some point we meet someone who suggests an idea that leads us to yet another location or action. Eventually it all falls into place. God seldom drops our next relationship on the front porch, but that can happen too. Another friend of mine was busy expecting her next boyfriend and ended up having a long-term relationship with the son of the man who did her landscaping. It was a hot day and the young man was already partially "unwrapped" to boot. That's a very special kind of consciousness in action!

Your Power Is Your Unique Expression Of Life

Do not wait for your dream to come true. Take action to begin immediately to create the life you want. If there are activities in your life that you can no longer tolerate then cut them out of your life. I would encourage you to heal the situation as best you can before leaving, because if we do not heal our wounds we are bound to repeat the same situation over and over again. On the other hand, spending time doing things we hate slowly kills us. If you really feel stuck in a situation of any kind you had better come to terms with it in some way, or you will pay the consequences and it will not be pretty.

Your health will suffer as a result of the stress you are putting on your body. Your emotional disposition will deteriorate so that no one will want to be around you. Besides killing yourself slowly, it doesn't do the rest of the planet any good either. This whole concept about discovering your life purpose (discovering what it is you do differently than anyone else) is about letting the rest of the planet benefit from your gift. If we are not giving of ourselves as we are uniquely qualified to do, then we are robbing the rest of the world of its good.

If what you're doing in the pursuit of your life purpose is truly unique, then no one else is going to be doing what you're doing exactly the way you do. If you intend to be a clinical psychologist then you will enroll in basically the same training all aspiring clinical psychologists take for at least the first four years of college. Then you will begin to specialize in a certain area of psychology, again along with other students and interns. Eventually, you will begin to set up your practice, most likely with another therapist in your area of interest with whom you have at least some basic agreement about modalities to utilize with patients. So how are you unique?

The way you interact with your patients and the areas in which you choose to concentrate are two ways that come to mind. The way you ultimately design and decorate your own office space when you set up your first private practice or the way you integrate your practice with that of other therapists are some other examples. At first, you will do it *The Way*, the way you've been taught. *The Right Way* will follow this, the methods that you have observed established successful clinicians using in operation. Eventually, if you expect to have far-reaching effects on the lives of your patients as well as enjoy the fulfillment of your own accomplishments, you will consider doing it *Your Way*.

Your Way will continue to incorporate some of *The Way* and *The Right Way* methods, but not all of them – only the ones that work for you. Doing it our own way first is what defines some people as the rebel or the know-it-all. This is the precise reason the educational system in the United States continues to be scrutinized. Our K through 12 school as well as the institutions of higher learning have for years prided themselves on getting students to think for themselves. In practice, however, the exact opposite is the case. The high school student who thinks for herself may be the student who finds herself in detention for breaking rules or marked down on citizenship for disagreeing with the teacher.

The latter of those two was my personal experience. *"Terry is a wonderful student and frequently surpasses my expectations. However* (there was *always* a "however" in the notes home to my parents)*, he needs to talk less, not ask so many questions, and stop correcting his teacher in front of the other students."* We are taught to follow the rules. This is a puzzling concept if society is going to grow since change cannot come about by doing the same thing over and over again. But often anyone who does not conform becomes the outcast.

Both doing it your way from the beginning, or starting off learning about the ways others do things, and then formulating your strategy based on your vision, are valid paths. I prefer a combination of both – much to the chagrin of my instructors in elementary school, high school, my graduate and post-graduate work, on-the-job training in various fields and ministerial training. I suppose I could have save space and your time by just saying I've been seen as a nonconformist throughout my life.

A more positive approach is to teach the rules but apply and follow them with principles. This is reflected in the Bible. The difference between the sections of the Bible has been described this way: The Hebrew (Jewish or Old Testament) Scriptures represent the law and the Greek/Aramaic (Christian or New Testament) Scriptures are the love. In the Hebrew Scriptures, Jehovah gave the nation of Israel strict laws to follow. Compliance guaranteed a reward; for disobedience, there were consequences. The same is true today:

We have freedom of choice, but not of consequence.

By making that statement I'm not predicting doom or punishment if we don't choose wisely. A consequence is not necessarily a negative event, though I suppose we more often than not use it that way. If I choose to plant my herb garden, water it and care for it the result (consequence) is that I should have a substantial storehouse of herbs till next spring, provided the rabbits don't "harvest" before I do. When we live our lives and make decisions from a foundation of choice (as opposed to obligation) we find freedom and empowerment instead of feeling like a victim when we agree to do something we really don't want to do,

When I began my ministerial training I was definite about how I wanted my ministry to look. I knew very well from being around other ministers and visiting other churches what I did *not* want it to look like. Plastic flowers with the visitor's gift packet were definitely out. That was cheap and tacky. Ranking right up there with plastic flowers were member's name badges – both smacked of little church and little church consciousness.

At the time I thought to be successful I would build a large church, so I wanted to act like it in my presentation to others. My instructor wanted her students to visit at least one church a month, inside and outside our denomination, and observe. She meant observe, not judge. At that time I was in high-bustle judgment mode. So God had a little Cosmic Giggle at my expense. You will not find it hard to believe that one of the brochure ideas I eventually added to my own church visitor packet was something I found in the visitor's gift packet with a tacky plastic flower taped to the outside! Just one more piece of evidence in my life that proves God *does* have a sense of humor.

Are You Having A Good Time?

Let's assume you have done everything possible to heal a difficult situation in your life. You begin to feel peace within yourself about the situation. At that point, ask yourself, "Am I having a good time?" If you are not having a good time doing whatever it is that you are doing, then why are you doing it? Does this mean we can have a good time all the time? Of course not.

We cannot have a good time 100 percent of the time any more than we can maintain a positive attitude 100 percent of the time. But we can have a good time most of the time and that certainly beats spending 90 or 95 percent of the time complaining about that five or ten percent of the time when life isn't the way we want it to be. We can even look for the joy in the sorrow. People are frequently surprised to hear me say that one of the things I find most rewarding in my ministry is officiating at a memorial or funeral.

It's not that I get some kind of charge out of the passing of someone from our earthly experience. The spouse, children, family and/or friends are sad. However, it gives me great personal satisfaction to know that in the midst of the grief I can exercise the power within me to comfort those people. In mentioning this to other ministers I find quite often that they feel the same way about these events.

We do not have answers to why one might have died so young or another suffered for so long, but we can be a presence of loving compassion to assist them in finding some answers within themselves. We can use our own past experience of overcoming indescribable and incredible grief to support them, letting them know they are not alone. It allows us to stand together through the confusion and questions as they discover their own answers. If they are willing, the event then becomes a celebration of life, instead of a mourning of death.

Giving Power To Fear

It takes a great deal of strength, a great deal of power, to move on in the face of fear and uncertainty. Moving on to a new job, a new city, a new relationship or a new way of life is a big step. It can be a simple step to take, though not necessarily easy. It may be exactly what you want to do and know you must do. It may also be a step for which you have little or no support from the others closest to you.

At this time it is as if we are standing on an Olympic diving platform. We know we must just jump off and do the particular sequence of twists and turns we have practiced over and over again. Only this time, it is from the highest platform. To make matters even more interesting, we may not even know if the pool has water in it, or if there is water, what the temperature is. We trust that the pool is full – after all, the contest was scheduled and people are in the stands – but we may stop ourselves at the last minute, or maybe not even climb the ladder. Why?

Fear. Fear is something to which most people give a lot of power. Fear stops us from going forward. It paralyzes us in our tracks. Fear, in and of itself, has no power. It only has as much power as we give it. Most of the time we not only give it the power, we steal power from other areas of our life and fuel the fear. There are two acronyms for the word *fear*. The more politically correct one is:

F alse E vidence A ppearing R eal

This is not to say that every fear we experience is based on false evidence. If a bus is careening down the street and headed directly for us then a certain measure of positive fear would be prudent in activating the appropriate chemical response to the situation and thereby giving us a greater physical ability to move quickly. One of the times our bodies produce additional adrenaline is during a time such as this, one precipitated by a fear response, where a danger exists.

The majority of our fears are based on false evidence, or perhaps more accurately *tainted evidence*. Aunt Ethel told us we would get cramps if we went swimming right after we eat, so even though there is no scientific evidence or much personal experience in the matter, we still wait that thirty minutes after the hot dog before we jump back in the surf because we are afraid Aunt Ethel just might be right. We do not apply for the job we really want because we are afraid that our résumé does not look as good as it should or that the company is not hiring our race-gender-sex-size-age. We decide not to ask that good-looking guy to dance because we fear he will say no, simply verifying our fear that we are too fat-thin-bald-gray-geeky-dorky-ditzy.

None of these fears are justifiable, yet we are faced with similar fears each and every day. Some we push through, like the year we finally push through our fear of that roller coaster we really wanted to ride year after year but have always been terrified to try. Others, such as a fear of what might or might not lie beyond the pain of leaving a physically-, sexually- or emotionally-abusive relationship are sadly not overcome, or perhaps overcome only when we are forced to make a life or death decision.

The other acronym, albeit less socially acceptable in most circles, more correctly describes my personal experience:

F *&#! E verything A nd R un

Scientists say that this reaction to a situation has its roots in our "fight or flight" response buried deeply within ancient instincts. The fear of facing what we do not understand, do not believe we can handle or do not wish to acknowledge, can make running away from the situation far more desirable than taking care of whatever it is.

We do not want to deal with the paperwork, legal proceedings and possible personal embarrassment of the sexual harassment, the rape or the slander. We walk away from the job, move out of the area or pretend like it didn't happen. We find an excuse to be anywhere in the world except back in our hometown for our twenty-fifth high school reunion because we just know everyone else there will be richer-happier-younger looking-more successful than we are. We feel frustrated and stuck, yet we are terrified to do whatever we need to do to change, usually because we are afraid that our situation might possibly get worse.

Change is necessary. Fear is one of the most powerful factors we allow to keep us from changing. <u>Fear does not stop us</u>. We *allow* fear to stop us. People fear change because even if the situation in which we find ourselves is far from ideal, at least it is familiar. My Grandma Esther used to say that it was like being up to your neck in horse manure. Eventually you get used to the smell and at least it's warm. The *warmth* of even the worst relationship or difficult job is that it is *familiar*. That familiarity is a sense of comfort to us even though it seems to run contrary to any logic given the circumstances. Here is how Ernest Holmes defined fear in his book, *The Science of Mind* (1938:156):

"...fear [is]... Nothing more nor less than the negative use of faith...faith misplaced;..."

Faith misplaced – we have faith that something is going to go wrong. With that attitude something probably will go wrong or we will make ourselves sick in the process. In cults, people are expected to believe what they are told to believe without any explanation and follow orders without question.

This type of blind faith based on credulity is not the type of faith we want to cultivate. The principles that govern the universe are laws that are immutable. They work the same way every time without regard to how they are being used or by whom they are being used. Having faith in the unsubstantiated fears of our lives, having faith misplaced, is the same as following a cult leader without question to our death.

The Apostle Paul told Hebrew Christians in the first century, *"Faith is the assured expectation of things hoped for, the evident demonstration of realities though not beheld."* (Hebrews 11:1, NWT) This scripture is usually quoted to remind Christians today to have faith in God during difficult times. It is just as applicable to our discussion about fear actually being misplaced faith. In its common usage we are reminded that in our past experience universal laws have worked efficiently.

That these laws have worked consistently in our lives is a firm foundation upon which to build our hopes for the present and future manifestation of our desires. The situation or outcome feared has not manifested, nor may we even have any concrete evidence that such will actually occur. Yet, we are exercising a powerful, anticipatory faith that disaster most certainly will befall us. In this way fear becomes a form of faith and a way of life.

The universal power available to us allows the building of our vision and creation of a life worth living. This same power can easily be redirected into the misuse of faith as fear. By standing up to our fears and acting in wisdom we overcome the fears and empower ourselves to continue towards the hopes, the dreams and the goals. The result is.

Fear of Success

Nearly three-quarters of a century ago, women were leaving the war factories to return to their homes and husbands to become the now legendary 1950s housewives. To think that their daughters would today be CEOs, airline pilots, military commanders, scientists, mayors, governors, firefighters, police officers and attorneys was unheard of. Most American mothers expected their daughters to follow in their footsteps. The next two decades would challenge our belief system as a nation and culture, giving birth to new opportunities for growth and fulfillment.

Many of our commonly held fears are carefully disguised in our belief systems. We must continually examine our core beliefs so that we might determine whether or not what we *say* we believe is truly what we *do* believe. Here is another fact that has received more and more attention in recent years: Beliefs that keep us small can come from our *fear of success* as well as our fear of failure.

It's been my experience that most of us are more terrified of succeeding than we are of failing. We may talk a lot about what we would like to have, but actually having it is another thing entirely. Large amounts of success can be unfamiliar and uncomfortable because it has not been our experience of the past. We begin to privately question what our new life will be like.

Will I lose my friends? Can I still go out to lunch with my old blue-collar group when I'm in management? What if people only like me for my money? I don't know if I can really handle all that money. The writer is afraid that if she has a successful first book then she'll have to have another one; or perhaps, she will have to be interviewed and she has stage fright – the first book never gets written, though you can be sure she will talk incessantly about writing that book. The father really wants to return to college and complete his degree, but the other students will be half his age or perhaps even his own children; other men his age have had their degrees for years; at his age what makes him think the company will promote him anyway—so Saturday mornings are spent cleaning the garage instead of attending weekend classes at the university.

The above so-called logical reasons are really just flimsy excuses for why we stop ourselves from succeeding. One school of thought says that you cannot fail if you do not try. But no matter how it turns out, you're never really a failure for trying. Personally, I would much rather give something my best shot than spend the rest of my life wondering if I could have done it, or complaining that I did not do it.

We never succeed or fail. We succeed or learn.

If we set out only to *try* (the implication that there is possibility for failure) then we ought not waste our time. But if we set out to *do* (implying that we already have the knowledge, understanding, wisdom and power to succeed) we have a much better chance of accomplishing that which we have set out to achieve. In practical terms, if an acquaintance responds to my invitation for dinner with, "I'll try to make it," I usually assume they are not coming. People who really want to get together with you will say so, not fain interest while waiting for a better offer.

Affirmations

One way to assist in the release of fear is by reprogramming our consciousness by the use of affirmations. Affirmations are short statements – positive and powerful – about a belief we want to establish within our conscious and subconscious thoughts. There are those in the New Age community who would have you believe that spouting affirmations with a smile on your face will solve all your problems, help you lose twenty pounds, find your perfect mate and win the lottery. This is what I like to call *pink cloud metaphysics*. The people who walk around with a perennial smile on their face characterize it. It is all show with no substance.

Make no mistake: Affirmations *alone* will not change your consciousness or situation. Affirmations must include the willingness on our part to change, to accept the new, to entertain at least a glimmer of hope that what we are beginning to consider just might somehow be possible. What is especially wonderful about affirmations is that we get to hear loudly what our subconscious really believes. The way this occurs is through the first thought we think or comment we make upon writing or speaking an affirmative statement.

We decide we want a mate in our life. We use the affirmation, *"I am attracting my perfect mate."* Instead of that warm fuzzy feeling we seek, a voice inside our head shouts, *"Oh yeah…right…like that last loser you picked! What makes you think you can do any better this time? You're just going to get hurt again…you watch!"* At that point we become rather startled. Where did all that come from? It came from the subconscious and just that one affirmative statement opened the floodgates of what has been stopping us from having what we want.

The challenge is to negate the objections and repeat the affirmations. The mistake people make is that they try to *ignore* the objections. If objections arise, deal with them. Ignoring them and pretending they aren't there is probably what we've been doing all along, which is just like the smelly elephant in the middle of the living room. Everyone sees it but no one wants to deal with it. If living a fulfilling life is to become a reality, then we have to deal with the smelly elephants that are living rent-free in our minds.

Here are a few ideas for changing negative thinking into a positive affirmation:

I don't know.

I make wise decisions.

I can't figure out what my purpose is.

I have a wonderful gift to give to life and I give it with joy!

I don't see how to get from where I am to where I see myself in my vision.

I know whatever I need to know to fulfill my vision.

Maintaining Our Power

Whenever we make a decision to change our thinking we are taking back the power to decide for ourselves how we want our life to be. It may take time. We did not instantly create the life we have now. Still, change is possible. On the brighter side, just because we have lived the way we have lived for ten, twenty or more years does not mean it must take the same amount of time for us to correct our belief system. If we take time to rejoice in the small accomplishments we will more quickly realize the larger ones, bringing us closer and closer to the life we envision for ourselves.

To do this means we must strive day in and day out toward our vision of life. We must maintain a steady flow of the power we've been discussing in this chapter so that we are moved along the path that we have chosen. The source of that power is unfailing and being consistently supplied to us. It is our choice whether or not to continue accessing that power source. The factor involved to maintain the desires that we have begun to realize is the topic of our next chapter: *Passion.*

Chapter Four

Passion

The word *passion* brings up all sorts of connotations. This word has a variety of meanings to people, just as the word elicited a wide range of responses. This is how people have responded when I asked them to define passion:

Love

Zeal

Lust

Erotic

Desire

Committed

Hot

Enthusiasm

Energy

Intensity

Do any of those surprise you? Do some of the words describe your feelings about passion? If you hear me make the statement "Those two sure are passionate together," you might think I have in mind two lovers. In fact, as I am writing this chapter, I am listening to a PBS presentation of a concert originally broadcast from Carnegie Hall in New York in 1995. The Boston Symphony, conducted by Seigi Ozawa, is performing an all-Tchaikovsky program. I have been watching Mr. Ozawa direct the orchestra, my surround-sound blaring out the open windows of my home on a most gorgeous day. I am a fan of Pyotr (Peter) Ilyich Tchaikovsky, perhaps because he and I shared some of the same struggles, perhaps because I remember my father listening to his music when I was a child.

The drive of the man, Tchaikovsky, gave birth to the music to which we listen today. It still causes tears in my eyes at times because of its intensely passionate energy and orchestral beauty. Mr. Ozawa's dedication to "playing" the orchestra and his love for what he presented in that recording was awesome. It is, therefore, not two lovers, but a long-dead Russian composer and a maestro born in Shenyang, China, about whom I am speaking.

Erotic Energy or Sexual Passion?

I strongly believe there is a very logical reason why Jane and Joe Public first associate passion with sex before almost anything else. As a culture of people, Western civilization hasn't got a clue how to use its erotic energy. Passion in the form of erotic energy springs from the core chakra, the Kundalini energy.

Unfortunately, when we feel this energy begin to stir as we enter puberty we are not given the guidance we need. This is not the fault of our parents; they probably weren't given the proper guidance either. Learning to channel this energy for uses other than sex and/or procreation is a key to becoming a more balanced individual in tune with the universe.

I am probably safe in saying most adults have experienced some sort of sexual and/or erotic gratification at some point in their life, however fleeting that might have been. It is then that we may have felt like we were one with a partner, or with everything around us. It is the feeling of being present where we are in the physical sense, yet present everywhere else at the same time. This feeling indicates that we are focused completely and totally in and on the moment.

That type of focus, or intense absorption in the moment, is passion. It is not confined to the bedroom, a quickie in the back seat, or to sex at all.

You may not have linked the passionate energy of a sexual experience to the good feeling you felt during a non-sexual time. The energy is the same; we just aren't taught to view it as such.

Think of another time when you were at one with the moment. Perhaps it was in a country field at night watching the stars. It could be in a musical setting, such as I felt with the symphony. It might be the subtle, yet glorious, colors of a Monet painting or the patriotic stirrings of a Fourth of July fireworks display. It is that, "God!-I-feel-like-I'm-going-to-burst-if-this-gets-any-better" feeling. *That* is the kind of passion you must generate in your life and living to experience satisfaction on an ongoing basis.

Is this too impossible to believe? It isn't so much that our lives become busy or that the fireworks display feeling is maintained at that level. No one lives life that way, even though it can appear to be so. It can wear me out just to watch Lady Gaga perform. She never seemed to stop! But Gaga cherishes her down time, rest and relaxation with her family when possible.

Life is ebb and flow. Just like the ocean, there is a current running constantly, high tide to low tide. It doesn't matter if our lives are running in high tide mode or low tide mode. There is a current running through us at all times. That current is the passion that drives us, empowers us and sustains us through the times of joy and celebration, as well as the other times.

Once again, affirmations can assist us in encouraging passion in our work. Here are some I have found useful and the meanings behind them:

I can be trusted.

This means I can trust *myself*. There is no one else I choose to trust more than myself. Even if that trust leads me to other people for counsel, I am capable of making my own decisions.

I am worth it.

It is okay to do things for myself. To do only for others, or others always first, only causes us to eventually resent those we serve. If it is really right for me, then everyone will be blessed.

I've got nothing to lose and everything to gain!

I'm here to celebrate and enjoy life.

Acting As If

A good question to ask at this point is, *Can I really just be totally in love with an idea, with a project – passionate about it?* This can be a great time to "act as if." Like affirmations, acting as if helps us to entertain new possibilities. We are taking an active part in visualizing ourselves in the situation we desire. It might even be a time to start building some of the foundation of our desire. On the other hand, if we ask ourselves the question above and we come up feeling empty, then perhaps we need to return to the basics in determining our true, passionate desire. We can't fake passion for very long. More importantly, why try?

I remember presenting seminar in Boise, Idaho, some years ago. During the break a woman named Pat came up to me, and explained she was moving closer and closer toward living her life purpose. When I asked her what it was, her face lit up, and she dove into her purse for a business card. This adult woman was almost giddy as she shoved the card into my hand. It was one of the most professional and beautifully printed business cards I have ever seen. She had selected a name which reflected her personality: warm yet businesslike, casual but not cutesy. Her business was private catering for small and large groups.

I asked her how long she'd been doing it and if she was doing it full-time. "Oh," she said, "I probably won't be starting up the business for another year or so. But I've got the cards for when I do!" That was acting as if, not to speak of being prepared for her good to manifest. I could *feel* her passion extending out from her to me and others nearby. I've never wanted a catering business, but I was ready to plan a party just so I could hire her!

Creating Privately, Quietly and Effectively

In most cases this process will be a very private and personal experience. When I was completing my ministerial training I was no more the pastor of a church than I was President of the United States. Still I spent a good deal of time at my computer creating a Sunday program, my newsletter, brochures, membership cards, a visitor's packet and class catalog. A "friend" criticized me for wasting time. He thought I ought to be out making money, volunteering somewhere or doing something "productive" instead of "wasting my time playing church." I quickly learned not to share my activities so freely. I continued to work on my future church.

By the time I got to Pittsburgh almost two years later, where I would open my first church, I only had to change the addresses of the classes and service locations. Everything was already done. I admit that I ended up changing the Sunday program a little each week for the first few months before I finally got it exactly the way I wanted it. But by honing my methods in the previous two years prior to beginning my ministry, I was "living as if" long before I attained that goal. In effect, I was two years ahead of the game because of "wasting time playing church."

Another way to put passion into your life is to see your dream or vision as a child. See it as an entity in and of itself, one that you are guiding, nurturing and helping to grow. As it begins to mature, you will no longer need to bottle feed it. It will begin to take on responsibilities, and a life of its own. You will move from a caregiver relationship to a relationship of mutual trust and partnership. Seeing your dream or vision as an entity, a life force of its own, helps remove some of the personal responsibility for *making* it happen.

It is our responsibility to do what is obvious for us to do. It is not our responsibility to push the river. Allow the dream (the vision) to draw to you all that it needs to fulfill itself through you. I like to picture it as a round ball – continuous, with no end. To embody our individual desires requires that we must disassociate ourselves from some of the "facts" and the way others do whatever they do while we are visualizing the final product or result. A favorite affirmation of mine for this is:

My vision (or dream) is complete in the Mind of God.

Here Comes the Fear!

You are not just a nothing in the Universe. You are IT! Get some attitude about yourself and your vision. You really are pretty wonderful and it is about time you started believing that so we can all enjoy the gift you have to give. You must not allow fear (of failure or of success) to slow you down, trip you up or stop you all together.

Is there something that scares you when you think about what you really want to do with your life? Great! If you weren't a little apprehensive there would be something wrong. A little positive recognition of the obvious dangers will help you avoid making foolish or perhaps even deadly mistakes. Once we recognize the fear we must follow the three steps below:

Examine it – Is this a valid fear? Is there anything to indicate you should really be afraid?

Deal with it – If it is a valid fear, then what can you do to change your circumstance or attitude? If it is not a valid fear, then why are you letting it stop you?

Forget it. Once you've dealt with it let it go. Period.

As you begin overcoming your fears, your logical considerations and the facts, passion takes over. This will give you energy and fires up the vision. It revitalizes your outlook. Does this mean you do not need a business plan? Does this mean you do not count the cost? No. But you also don't waste time worrying about solving problems that can only occur after Step 25, whatever that might be in your plan, when you haven't even taken Step 1 toward your vision.

It is as if you want to learn how to pilot an airplane, but refuse to sign up for flight lessons because you do not know how you'd handle flying in dense fog by instruments alone. It is not calling the State for forms to register your business because you do not have the money to incorporate. The knowledge to fly by instruments, the money to incorporate or the right person to keep your books will show up when it is needed. If we are passionate about our desires the universe will magnetically draw that which we need to us without fail. Remember:

That which you desire also desires you.

The Vision and the Mission

I have used the word *vision* at various times in this book. I believe everyone needs a vision *and* a *mission*. Other teachers and methods use the word "mission" for what I call a vision, so I want you to understand clearly how I define these terms in my work and in this book so that we may proceed. Here's the way I see the difference.

The vision statement is the *what*, the basic feeling you want to achieve in your life, or a certain area of your life. By certain area, I mean you will have a life vision, but can also have a career vision, a relationship vision with your partner or spouse, and many others. We can have a variety of visions that are specific to various areas of our life, which support the overall vision of what we want our life to be.

While the vision statement is the what, the mission statement is the *how* of the process, the doing part, the numerous experiences which make up our life path on the earthly plane. The mission is the guide to day-by-day operation, seeing our life becoming what we want to feel from our vision. That can be a pitfall if we are not careful. How I think my plans should work out and how Divine Mind sees it may not always agree. God always has the better idea – not necessarily of the what, but the how.

Like the vision, the mission must not be so specific that it eliminates our growth. One minister I know simply has "For support, call..." on her business cards. She serves people in a variety of ways. She once told me she didn't have the foggiest idea *how* to serve others, she was just *there* to serve. As she has opened herself up to be of service she has not only helped others over the years but has also widened her experiences.

If you are in a love relationship or business relationship with someone else, the two (or more) of you can have a vision and mission for that relationship. Just like the various areas of our own personal lives complement our vision for life, our joint visions and missions with others enhance our own life vision and mission.

Your vision statement is what you feel your purpose is in life. It should be short, clear and, most important of all, *personal*. Vision and mission statements should each be one or two sentences long at the very most. Some other methods of designing a vision or mission teach people to create much longer statements. Some organizations go on for a full page or longer. This method smacks of ego and the need for approval.

The finished product looks great on a wall plaque near the elevator, but most of us do not have elevator lobbies in our homes. Your business plan belongs in a notebook, not in your mission statement. If you have rules, regulations and principles for operating, they belong in your Policy and Procedures manual, not in your vision statement. Keep it simple. This is something you want to be able to easily memorize and think about throughout the day.

Creating your vision and mission statements is going to take some time. Meditate on them. Pray about them. It may take up to six months of writing, re-writing, pondering, changing, and tweaking before you get a statement which really feels like it is right...or you might already know what it is. You must decide intuitively and deeply within yourself what feels right for you. It is not a left-brain, analytical exercise. This is a right brain, emotionally based, intuitive exercise. (Note: For additional suggestions on becoming more clearly focused on your vision and life purpose, see the exercise *Creating the Vision* in the Appendix of this book.)

How to Create Your Vision and Mission

The following method is helpful in creating a vision and mission statement for one's life. It is the method I use when working with groups and organizations to formulate vision and mission statements. Clear off the kitchen table or push aside the couch and get down on the living room floor. Put on some music to really get you excited about what you are doing.

This might be meditative music along with candles and incense, or it could be a dance track with flashing lights. It is your vision, your mission and your life – it is about time you started having fun with it! Get two large sheets of butcher or freezer paper. Grab some colorful pens or markers. Write "Vision Statement" at the top of one sheet. Write "Mission Statement" on the top of the other. Set the mission sheet aside and start on the vision sheet.

Write down on the vision sheet all the feelings you want in your life. Allow your mind to flow and write without analyzing your thoughts. Let intuition guide you in using particular colors for particular words. Drawings or even doodling may appear, perhaps more accurately expressing the feeling you wish to experience. Take at least fifteen minutes on this section to start. In a group situation this takes most of the afternoon, so do not rush the process.

Next, on the mission sheet, write down all the things you like to do that result in those feelings. This may be more difficult. Perhaps you are working hard all the time and do not have a lot of playtime or fun activities, in which case this part may feel like a dead end. Should this section give you any trouble, begin to explore how you might actually experience your vision. Let your mind go and see just how willing you are to have your life work the way you want it to work. Later on, I will show you how to explore these possibilities. This will enable you to fine-tune your statements.

Again, I remind you that you are just beginning this process. If we are to live the lives we want then we must be patient. Some areas will be created easily and quickly. Others take time. It took me almost a year to come up with my original statements. That doesn't have to be everyone's experience. It indicates to me just how off course I was at the time. Each of us must allow ourselves to grow through this process without judgment or comparisons. Here are the original vision and mission statements that guided my life for a number of years:

My vision is to live an abundant, peaceful life in an atmosphere of joy, love and playfulness.

My mission is to help others create a life worth living by being powerful and loving.

That's it. Simple. Brief. And packed full of more work and commitment than I ever thought possible. People who honestly believe that their heart's desire has always been to save the world think my vision and mission are pretty odd. This isn't about the world. *It is about each of us individually,* even though living our personal statements affects the entire planet.

Many people do not think a whole lot about themselves. Most people criticize themselves more than anyone else in their life. We are the person who we usually put last. Guess what? That's all old news. It is time for *you* to be happy. It is time for *you* to have what you want. It is time to start taking better care of *yourself* than you ever have up until now.

That is not selfish. It is not even ego-based. It is the foundation of having a life worth living. Did you read the title of this book? It is not *Get Your Mother's Life For You*, or *Get the Life You Think God Wants You to Have So You Will Get Into Heaven*. This is about what *you* want. Those who criticize this philosophy will scurry off to a dark corner like little rodents to make sure their stuff is secure. They will talk about you and complain to each other about how awful their lives are. Let them. It is better for them to be off making themselves more miserable and out of your space. That's apparently what they want, so let them be.

As I said earlier, the vision and mission statements above were ones that guided my life for a number of years, nearly thirty actually. Just recently it became necessary to alter them slightly to more closely fit my current goals and life path. The original ones were adapted to the following:

My vision allows me to live an abundant, peaceful life in an atmosphere of love, joy and playfulness.

My mission helps me assist others in creating lives worth living by being a powerful and loving leader.

One of the changes you may have noticed is that the form of the verb "to be" has been eliminated in the revised statements. By removing "is" from the statements the active verb "allows" and the phrase "helps me assist" produces even more power to the vision and mission. You might want to read each form for yourself and see how they feel for you. Does one or the other create within you a more powerful experience? If so, that may help you in the development of your own vision and mission statements.

Here's what happens when you start living your life the way you know you want to live it: You become happy. Guess what type of person you are to be around? You are a happy person. Miserable people want to share their misery. They cannot wait for you to get down with them in the mud and roll around bitching, pissing, moaning and whining about how awful life is.

On the other hand, the happy person wants to help other people be happy. Other people helped me have the life I have: fulfilling, abundant, loving and satisfying. My life is unfolding perfectly. In the process I'm blessed to get to help others. You will too.

Identifying the Obstacles

Obstacles will come up. No road is without a few bumps, a winding curve or two and the occasional detour. When the obstacles arise, look to see what might really be the root of the problem. Be aware of what is under that fear.

One of the biggest fears that we secretly harbor is the fear that we have made a mistake. We *should* have taken the job. We *should* have known better. We come down with a dose of the "shoulda-wouldas." What we should have done is exactly what we did do given where we were in consciousness at the time. *What we would have done is irrelevant since we didn't do it and have no means to go back to prove that we would have done what we now think we should have done.*

Go back and re-read that last sentence. Ponder it. Study it. Believe it. If you want to read more about this principle, refer to the Suggested Reading section in the back of this book for information on a novel by Dr. Wayne Dyer, *Gifts from Eykis.*

These thoughts of fear and doubt are normal and natural to a certain extent. This is particularly true whenever we are out charting new territory and attempting to do things we've not done before. Each of us must analyze whether these concerns are passing thoughts to be considered or serious revelations of impending doom. A measure of rational concern or doubt can amount to merely planning for various alternatives. It is what the Scriptures refer to as building on a solid foundation rather than shifting sands (Luke 6:49). We must take a serious look at our faith in the Power within us if every obstacle becomes evidence to us that we are unworthy, about to fail or should never have even begun.

The more positive and productive alternative to the "shoulda-wouldas" is the "mighta-couldas". Instead of thinking we should have done this or would have done that, we see obstacles as a means to learn a better course of action that we *might* or *could* utilize now or in the future. If some plan falls through before our eyes we can take the time to examine why. Without making ourselves wrong and beating ourselves up we can objectively look at what we might have done differently, and what we could change in our approach or thinking to avoid the same situation again.

One of the definitions of insanity is doing the same thing over and over again and expecting different results. To affect change in our lives we can be willing to approach obstacles in our path with an open attitude of learning, humility and childlike amazement. Only then can we expect to open our consciousness to the intuition provided abundantly through us by Divine Wisdom.

Prosperity

Obtaining your vision does not have the hidden agendas of acquiring fame or fortune. Living the vision may very well, and many times does, include these things and more, but that is not the driving force. The attitude about doing what you love to do and seeing the financial reward as a result is a sound one. It is just that seeing the financial reward is not the reason for doing what you love to do. You do what you love to do because you enjoy it. I write because I love to write. Occasionally what I write gets read by someone else and that person is benefited in some way. At times I'm paid well for my published work. But, the public will never read the majority of what I write. If I only wrote for money I would not be writing much.

Never, never, never work for money. Work at what you love to do (or at what you can love while you are creating the work you desire) and expect to be paid well for what you are doing. The late Dr. Juanita Dunn was a well-known spiritual counselor and minister. Her counsel was in very high demand. She mentored and advised many prominent people in this country. In one of the classes I took from her during the beginning of my ministerial training she said this about work and money: "I do not work for money. I work. Therefore, I have money." By this Dr. Juanita meant working at what she loved to do – in her case, teaching and doing pastoral counseling.

That wisdom made a tremendous impact on how I would live my life over the next few years as a self-employed person. If you are drawing a paycheck for the work you do 40 hours a week, that money will be there whether you like your job or not. Some days you may not enjoy it, other days you might. Either way, you get paid. I realize that if you continually do not enjoy it you will be making yourself sick or get fired, but stay with me for a minute here. That scenario is somewhat different if you are self-employed – or at least it can look that way.

Suppose you are living your dream and that dream is painting houses. You work for yourself and you love it. An apartment building owner, who has hired you before, approaches you with a business proposition. It just so happens that your job assignments have slacked off recently. This woman is offering you the opportunity for an exclusive contract to keep her complexes painted. The money is good. The consistency of work is assured. There's just one problem. You really do not get along with this woman. She wants you to use cheap materials. She only wants white paint. She's faultfinding.

You have a decision: 1) Turn her down because she's a royal pain in the butt, and no amount of money is worth the abuse you will have to endure; or 2) Take the opportunity to have a steady income regardless of the cost. I have chosen both of those paths at various times. When I chose option number one, I found myself feeling empowered and clean.

Almost without fail, I have had new doors of opportunity open to me in a matter of days. Choosing the other path was almost always a disaster. I felt imprisoned, used and like a victim. Working for money will allow that to happen. Rev. Edwene Gaines is a Unity minister whose prosperity and commitment seminars are known worldwide. As I once heard her say, "Sugar, working for money is the oldest profession in the world, so you might as well call it what it is!"

Why Do You Have To Do It?

If you want to become an actor, singer, minister or flight attendant, any person in any of those fields will tell you, without a moment's hesitation, that if there is anything else you can do or want to do other than become involved in their career then you should most certainly do it. Why? It is not because these are awful, terrible careers. I have undertaken each of these careers at some point in my life. I am currently pursuing two of them. Then why would I or anyone else in these fields suggest something else for you when we are so in love with what we do?

Because each of these careers, as well as many others, requires a time and lifestyle commitment most people are unwilling and/or unable to handle. If you are serious about living your life purpose, about finding and living your vision, you must ask yourself: Why? Answers such as "I just have to," "I've always wanted to," or even "I feel it's my calling" may not stand the test of time in my experience. Those reasons may make people sigh and smile at how brave and certain you sound. But, in my opinion, it can also be a bit of an "airy fairy" response to which we are attracted because of exactly the response it elicits from others. Without knowing why, passion is not possible.

It takes little if any passion to show up at work on time, complete our job, collect a paycheck and go home. All we are doing is following orders. Living our vision is far more than this. But first, consider the common 9-to-5 routine. A 40-hour per week job with two weeks of vacation every year might be just what one person needs to provide financial regularity in her or his life. This situation allows their vision to unfold without regard to monetary needs. A full- or part-time job working for someone else can allow us the free time to pursue activities in support of the vision. You might recall my own experience related earlier in this book about my work as a legal secretary while building my first church; and, how that job benefited not only me, but my ministry as well. In this sense, the job, even if it is not particularly interesting, becomes part of the foundation in building the vision and seeing its fulfillment.

Without passion, the uninteresting or boring job is perceived as just that, uninteresting and boring. We may even begin to resent having to be on the job, become critical of our boss or fellow workers, and ultimately create life-threatening stress in our lives. What is the difference since we are discussing the same exact job? The difference is passion. A person can go to work just to obtain money to survive. In doing so, the job becomes their passion – actually forcing themselves into a life-pursuing activity in which they have little or no interest.

The person who works at a job for the purpose of supporting a larger vision has little or no difficulty in doing the work because it is just one small component in a much grander idea. For centuries religious devotees have joyfully performed menial tasks in monasteries, convents and ashrams because their work was part of the bigger picture. There can be no questioning of the task when the purpose is one of passionate, committed intention. Without being passionate about your vision you will only be obsessed with reaching goals or staying busy.

It becomes evident that passion is vital for the person who intends to be self-employed through the day-to-day operation of their vision. To rely on the universe as truly our only Source, and to be unswervingly clear in our commitment to our vision, requires a tremendously strong conviction that we have what it takes to do whatever is necessary to live our dream. Passion must be the driving force behind us, day after day, week after week and year after year. Even though passion must be present for success there is a danger. That danger is thinking another activity is passion when it is not. There is a destructive, driving force that in today's society frequently masquerades as passion.

Obsession is not passion.

Learn this. Know this. Do not be fooled into thinking that just because you are staying busy it means you are accomplishing anything more than staying busy. Writers are one group of artists who are often guilty of obsession. Writers frequently spend more time organizing their writing than actually writing. They set up manila folders or computer files, sub-files and sub-files for their sub-files. They gather books for research, piling them up all over their work area, which is exactly where the books stay, unopened and gathering dust, but providing the convincing illusion that they are very, very busy doing something.

Artists can become so obsessed with expressing themselves that the writer does not write, the painter does not paint and the sculptor does not sculpt. Why? They have become obsessed with the doing of the work instead of passionate about their expression. There is an easy way to find out if you are obsessed by your vision or passionate about it.

Obsession is your purpose if at the end of the day you are exhausted to the point of pain, angry about life and with your mind still racing. The passionate person has had just as much if not more activity during the day, but ends the day with a peaceful satisfaction, looking forward to both a night of rest and the new day ahead to move closer toward the vision.

It is imperative that we see the value in what we do. If you can do something better than anyone else, appreciate that. Release any thought that acknowledging your magnificence is egotistical. If you are not doing what you think you ought to be doing, begin with doing the very best at what you *are* doing. Continue to see your worthiness for obtaining your vision. Be willing to accept success.

As you continue to work on your vision and mission statements circumstances will change. You are putting a universal law into motion. Expect results. Opportunity never stops knocking. However, frequently we stop responding. If you find your prayers being answered or the right person shows up at the right time resist the temptation to say, "This is too good to be true." Instead, replace that with, *"This is good enough to be true."*

Visualizing the Goal or Limiting the Vision?

My clients often ask me whether or not they should visualize their vision. Visualization is highly effective for hopes, dreams and goals. When you are talking about a vision, visualization can be somewhat limiting. Remember that when we are visualizing, we are being very specific about what we want. While it can assist us with clarity in any given situation it can also amount to outlining to the universe exactly how our desires shall be made manifest. This can be exactly what you want to do, or it can be an attempt to redirect divine intelligence.

Our visions are greater than we can conceive of at any given moment. This is not necessarily true of our goals, as goals are smaller than the vision. The cycle is circular, with the vision at either the top (seeing it as that for which we are striving) or at the bottom (seeing it as the basis, the foundation of all we do). Use whichever position has more meaning for you. Proceeding from the vision are our dreams. Dreams are sometimes logical, sometimes off-the-wall.

It does not matter. We can dream whatever we want to dream. Dreaming is fun and opens our conscious and subconscious minds to possibilities. Some of those dreams are realistic enough to us that we truly hope the dream will come true. As the hope becomes stronger we take positive action through setting goals. Then, plans of action result in the goals being reached. As more and more goals are reached, the hope becomes attainable, the dream becomes fact and we find ourselves living a happier life by coming closer to our vision.

Become passionate with your vision. Only you can create the excitement of passion in your life that is sustainable and reliable. Classes are great, seminars are wonderful, self-help books are enlightening, but when it comes right down to it, it all comes back to you. You can take as many classes, and seminars as you can afford and then some. You can workshop yourself into a stupor. You can buy every purple outfit there is to announce your spiritual enlightenment, search out every possible piece of crystal jewelry and burn sandalwood incense till smoke fills your house, and it still comes down to you. None of any of that will mean anything if you cannot feel the passion for your vision.

One of the most passionate ways I've found to express this is in something written by Ernest Holmes in his book, *This Thing Called You* (1948):

"It is not necessary to spend your entire time in prayer and meditation. Rather, seek to make your work a prayer, your believing an act, your living an art. It is then that the object of your faith will be made visible to you. It is then that you shall kiss the lips of your desire."

How would it be to "kiss the lips of your desire?" How would it be to see your vision come alive through your mission? By developing a passion for our vision and mission we begin to experience the fulfillment of those things, a profound sense of peace, centeredness, joy and abundance. In other words, we are achieving a life worth living.

Receiving the Rewards

To be truly abundant and liberally rewarded in our daily life both spiritually and materially we must be willing to give to others and ourselves. If you want a really big gift, then you must be willing to receive a really big reward in return. Perhaps your gift will not come from the persons to whom you give, but the law of circulation is dependent on giving *and* receiving. One cannot be absent from your life without that same life in some way becoming out of balance. Here are some affirmations along this line:

I am open to experience all that is right for me.

Being open to experience *everything* may produce more than you bargained for.

I am open to receive   (fill in the blank)   .

Decide what you want to receive. Just being "open to receive" is not enough – particularly if our consciousness still has within it a recess or two that says we deserve to receive punishment or guilt for some success or desire. Get the picture?

As we are changing our belief systems and way of life, old attitudes and thought patterns may occasionally re-surface. At times these can show up as other people in our lives. If jealous, nasty or disbelieving people appear before you, know that they are there to mirror your own doubts. Treat them with respect and honor, because their opposition makes you aware of what it is you must be working on next. It is a big step to take responsibility for your life. Understand this is your choice, but not necessarily the choice of everyone else in your life.

Many people drift aimlessly through life saying they are waiting upon the Will of God. My theological belief is in a power that I call God (Goddess, Spirit, Divine Presence, or any number of other names and terms depending on my mood and needs) that responds to our desires in accordance to our willingness and capability to accept. In this context, the Will of God *is* my will, as long as my desires are not in conflict with immutable universal laws.

There is another type of will and that is willpower. The Will of God is the natural flow of the universe. It supports us in achieving our vision. Any focused, definite direction we give our lives could be considered willpower. That is a quality which gives Spirit the ability to act on our desires. There is another kind of willpower that ought not to be mistaken for spiritual direction. It is when our ego mind begins to run out of control and attempts to manipulate or focus the circumstances before us.

This works about as well as trying to get heat in your car while you're running the air conditioning. This form of willpower is not conducive to a happy life. This is another reason why visualization (as compared to visioning) can at times actually delay our good. Visualization takes a tremendous amount of focused energy. Visioning is a process that this book doesn't delve into, but requires a complete and total release to being inspired without the confines of specific requirements.

Can we use the power of our minds to force our desires into manifestation? Can we visualize desires so that they materialize in some particular way? Yes. I recommend that if you use this method you are crystal clear about that which you desire and the price you may have to pay for the result. If you choose to do this you have a great possibility of success, but because it will be your willpower that creates the situation, it must also be your willpower that sustains it until such time as your manifestation melds into the flow of Spirit. This is exhausting. If we are not absolute on our intention we can also very quickly end up losing the situation we have manifested. The person to whom this happens then usually blames God or someone else. It is really pretty disempowering in the end.

At various times in my life I have confused focus with willpower. We forget from time-to-time that we are just one expression of infinite wisdom. When this occurs we see ourselves as separate and individual. We begin to suppose it's "All up to us." This leads to our clear focus becoming clouded with self-righteous willpower. I would like to have described those times as being intensely focused, but to be honest it would have to be more accurately expressed as sheer willpower wielded through belligerent force and egotistical self-importance. By visualizing with a relaxed and confident attitude, our desires will manifest in divine right time and order, and be sustained by an omnipotent Power that never needs to rest.

We have discussed the *Possibility* of creating a life worth living. We have looked at the Divine *Power* at our disposal. In this chapter we learned more about what it means to have *Passion* for our desires and life. Next, we will cover the reason that many people begin to have the life they want only to lose it. One of the most difficult tasks we have in life is to keep doing the inner work we know we must do on ourselves. To do that takes *Practice*.

Chapter Five

Practice

Practice is an ongoing process. This chapter can be a reference guide to assist you in creating the vital daily methods necessary to realize your unique expression of life. The exercises included are thought-provoking, challenging and infinitely rewarding. Take your time in completing them. Begin with the exercise you are most drawn to and incorporate it in your daily practice. When you are ready to add another, or go onto another, do so. This is not a test, just like life is not a test. Challenging our beliefs is part of the process by which we grow. These exercises are an example of what revolves around the *practice* of living a life of happiness and fulfillment.

Life is a journey, not a destination.

My father taught me to read music and to play the trumpet before I entered kindergarten. My grandma Esther taught me to play the piano beginning in the first grade. While I struggled, they always made playing their instruments of choice look so easy. It looked easy for them because they practiced those instruments for years before I was born. Think of a person you know or admire, someone whom you believe lives a fulfilling life or existence. They make it look easy, don't they?

It is their consistent, positive attitude and ease with life that draws us to them. If you ask anyone like this, or anyone successful, you will find that their situations may have been different not very long ago. They achieved their bliss and level of success by practicing diligently in the areas in which they knew they must improve or educate themselves. They didn't stop there. Each day they continue to hone their skills and abilities, learn new ways of accomplishing their desired results and constantly educate themselves in new arenas.

Many children today are still being taught that the end result is more important than the effort and experience that brings about the result. It is in the doing of any endeavor that we can find the most satisfaction. By rushing through the process, whatever the situation, we bypass the joy of the undertaking, the work or even the difficulty. We can easily arrive at the completion with no real enthusiasm with regard to celebrating our victory. It is common for many people to nearly ignore their own accomplishments as they hurriedly climb the next mountain, pursuing the next goal.

Celebration and Mourning

We get stuck in the process because we do not complete endings. We need to celebrate and mourn the completion of our goals before we attempt something new. The mourning is just as important as the celebration. Acknowledging and appreciating our accomplishments is apparent. We have hoped for the desired outcome, dreamed about it, visualized it as being a reality, set goals to bring us closer to the end result and followed through on those plans to such an extent that we are now reaping the benefits of our labor.

The mourning of which I am speaking is usually not so apparent. The most common example is finishing our schooling. After seven years of ministerial school I was certified and qualified to go out into the field and take on the responsibilities of a pastor for a church. This was an exciting time in my life, one I had looked forward to for some time. It would not appear that I had much to mourn about. The act of mourning is precipitated by a loss.

In my case, and in the case of anyone studying for any period of time, the loss is of no longer being in school. For seven years I talked about what I was going to do – now I was faced with doing it. Talking about doing anything and actually doing it are two very different things. How many times have you heard a co-worker complain again and again about their job? They repeatedly say how this time is that last straw, this time they are going to re-write their résumé and they are out of there. That kind of person seldom leaves. It is far easier to complain about our lives than actually do something about it.

More Fear of Success

My mourning for the loss of student status was short-lived when a more seasoned minister reminded me that as the pastor I was required to be not only the best practitioner of our teachings but also the best ongoing student. When I recognized that I was going to be in front of the class doing the educating as a teacher more often than being in a seat and listening as the student I had to acknowledge something else: I had accomplished my goal. I was recognized as a minister. Once I recognized myself as a minister, I was led to the next step on my spiritual path. That step took the form of a question, the answer of which was somewhat of a mystery to me at the time. That question in my life was the same one for any one of us when a project is completed or a goal realized:

Now what do I do?

We do not always want to acknowledge the endings because we're afraid of the new beginning. Many times we appear to go backward or stand still because of the fear of moving forward. Some people stay in school for many years, getting yet one more degree. It isn't a degree that is going to make us happy or successful. The same is true for more money, the right car, the perfect mate or the best location for our home. Our happiness, success, satisfaction and the ability to experience bliss depend primarily on our own attitude about our talents and our commitment to our vision.

Moving Beyond the Accomplished Goal

One way to get beyond this barrier and move forward is the fourth step, Practice. By practicing the principles of success in our lives we open ourselves to more and more of the good we say we want. Rev. Edwene Gaines once said that every time her life gets better than she thought possible, it seems that God somehow opens another door and things get even more exciting and rewarding. This caused her to coin the phrase that she must "increase her tolerance for pleasure."

We all say we want to have wonderful lives, full of love, prosperity, perfect health and satisfying careers, yet a closer examination finds most of us ill prepared to accept such magnificence. The philosophy of "Wait till the other shoe drops" or "This is too good to be true" permeates our culture. I'm not entirely sure where the concepts came from originally, though much of our Western agreement in this area comes from the Dark Ages.

This was a time in history when the Church and the State realized they could subjugate the common people through religious guilt, physical threats and false promises. The majority of the people were illiterate. Common folk innocently gave away their fortunes and lives to the Church to protect them from the Devil or buy their way into heaven. They bowed to the State expecting protection from invading armies. They blindly believed that the educated religious leaders and royalty knew what was best for them.

Today many people still seem to have adopted this rather perverse dichotomy of wanting more and at the same time feeling like they should have only what they have or even less. It is not only counterproductive but it is also extremely stress-producing. The holy writings of most cultures teach us that there is a Power greater than us. This Power expresses Itself through Its creations. It is there to support us. It is up to us to open to the possibility of being supplied abundantly all of the time, in all areas of our lives.

Exercise #4 - What Do You Want?

For this exercise I suggest using a yellow, legal-sized pad. The important factor here is that you have plenty of room to write. Set a timer for five minutes. Write down every desire you have – do not question it, do not edit your list, do not ask how, do not ask why, do not ask where and above all: <u>Do</u> <u>Not</u> <u>Judge</u> <u>Your</u> <u>Desires!</u> Keep writing until the full five minutes is up. Then move into Exercise #5.

Exercise #5 - Our Feelings About Success

For our hopes, dreams and goals to become realities, both our conscious and subconscious mind must be able to accept those realities. Read back through the list you just created – one item at a time. Start with the first item. Accept that item as already yours. For the sake of an example let's say that the first item was a new car. Speaking out loud and say, "I have a beautiful new car!", then write a few lines about what immediate thoughts popped into your head.

Perhaps you will think, "YES! It is dark blue with black leather interior, a top-of-the-line sound system synched with my mobile devices, and a sunroof." Or, you may find a little voice saying, "Yeah, right…like you're going to pay hundreds of dollars more a month for a new car you do not need and cannot afford. Who do you think you're kidding?"

These two exercises are not ones you should complete quickly. Allow yourself the luxury of time and then enjoy the benefits of working on the only person who can truly make a difference in your life: You.

Believing In Your Success

Our goals should cause us to stretch; otherwise the accomplishment of the goal may be less than fulfilling. It is helpful, at first, when we are setting goals, to set ones that we honestly believe are attainable.

A long-time goal of mine has been to have my own jet. It has never been at the top of my current list, since I've always been clear that I have no mental equivalent of being able to manifest that goal in the near future. I haven't intended to work at making that goal a reality at this time. It has been one of my dream goals, a fantasy of sorts, something I've always thought would be a hoot to have and something that brought a smile to my face.

I first placed that goal on my sheet of goals and desires in the mid-1980s. Back then I had the "yeah, right" attitude about it, but it stayed there, though the size of the aircraft continued to increase as newer models became available in the aviation industry! I knew inside, if I really wanted it, I could have it. I just didn't see any way that it could happen. Still, I would get a giggle out of thinking of all the cool things I could do with it: Fly my dad out to California for the weekend to see his grandchildren; pick up my mom while I was out there and do Hawaii for the weekend; stop in San Francisco to shop; then maybe load everyone up and go to London overnight for a show and dinner the next day before returning home.

Outrageous? Not really. Plenty of people have their own jets. No one in my immediate family or circle of friends at this time has their own private jet, but that doesn't mean it is beyond the realm of possibility. Is it a truly believable scenario or even probable in my consciousness as I write this chapter? The answer may surprise you as it did me. In the time that it took from beginning to teach this process in seminars to getting the material into book form, the answer changed.

The answer to that question in the early 1990s when I first taught my seminars using the principles in this book was, "No." I originally used this illustration to help identify desires we might have in our dreams, but that were not yet part of our consciousness. I wanted my students to choose items and experiences they thought were truly possible and probable, just not in their lives at that particular time. I was afraid that if they chose to place those types of goals at the top of their lists they would be quickly disappointed, since they would not at the time possess the mental equivalent of that goal.

It has now been several years since I began to expand and supplement this project into book form. Not only has the answer turned to "Yes," but something even more remarkable has occurred: I got the jet! It isn't *my* jet, but as employee of a major airline my job allows me the opportunity to travel for pleasure, either free or at a drastically reduced fare. These benefits apply to my immediate family and friends as well.

If my mother wants to visit me for a day or two, she does. If I wanted to see my family on the west coast, I do. I no longer *wish* I could travel where I desired. I can, and have, gone to Europe for the weekend on several occasions. It's now a situation of deciding where I want to travel and carving out the time to go, but I don't spend time trying to decide whether or not I can actually do it.

Originally another way I used this example was to encourage my students to put seemingly outrageous desires on their lists, but not as main goals, just for the fun of it. For this to be effective, however, listing outrageous desires should only be added to the main list if they bring a smile to our face. If we digress into a feeling that we can't ever have it or don't deserve it, best to leave it off the list. The lesson here to be learned is that Spirit feels *all* of our desires, no matter how outrageous.

I thought I needed my own jet. Instead, I get to use one in a fleet of about 900 jets when I need them, and leave all the maintenance and lease payments to a major corporation that can well afford them. Other desires on my running list have manifested in much the same way. In some cases, I'd forgotten that I'd even written down some items. It is only when I take time to review my list periodically that I realize I already have something I didn't even expect! This is proof positive that while I'm busy doing what I think I need to do to accomplish my current goals, Spirit is in the background, like a hidden algorithm in a computer program, busily and efficiently taking care of business, working on all sorts of projects not currently in my present scope of focus.

Once we get the hang of this something extraordinary can occur. I was presented a while back with a beautiful, engraved pocket watch by a friend as a token of her thanks for assisting her with a project. A silver pocket watch has *never* been on my master list, yet it is something I have often admired and thought, "Gee, I'd love to have one of those."

Spirit picked up those repeated, casual thoughts, without any coercion on my part and without any list making or intense visualization. It is a beautiful timepiece, more beautiful than I have seen in the past and even has Roman numerals on the face instead of digits – another preference of mine for a watch! I don't know about you, but I find this as amazing and fascinating as I do comforting and assuring. Or, as my mother once said:

"Isn't it interesting how life happens while we're living it?"

Possibility and Probability

For our goals to be fulfilled, our mind must be convinced not only of the *possibility* but of also the *probability* of success. Possibility has much to do with faith in ourselves and believing there is a universal power on our side. Probability is more about the beliefs and opinions we currently hold, or have held in the past, of our lives and ourselves.

A person who is seeking a life mate and yet continually puts himself or herself down has little chance of finding the partner they claim to seek. Another person may dream of being a college professor teaching high-level courses but does not possess the credentials and degrees necessary for such a position, making any attempt at applying for such a position a losing proposition. We must have the belief and complete faith in our ability to accomplish the goal.

This is why it is easy to become discouraged with creating lists of what we say we want. We may not really believe that attaining some material possessions is really possible. We may not have faith that our life can change or even work at all. It is like trying to manifest a Mercedes on a Kia consciousness. There's nothing wrong with having a Kia or a Mercedes or any other car we want. But we must have the mental equivalent of our desire and the consciousness to accept it.

I remember attending a seminar about prosperity years ago. A woman there who did not have a job or a permanent home placed a gold Rolls Royce at the top of her list. To my knowledge she did not obtain one. For her it wasn't the car, it was the attitude of being wealthy that she wanted. But for the few years I knew her I never saw any real progress toward her goals.

There are two major reasons why that was true for her. The first was that she did not really believe it was possible. The second was that she believed that having money and possessions were the keys to prosperity. Material abundance is not the source of anyone's abundance, though it can be a demonstration of prosperity. It is fun to dream all we want about paying cash for the jet or the Rolls. It is just a good idea to be sure we can pay the rent first.

How Is None Of Our Business

Even with all the training necessary for a job or all the inner work being done, we can still doubt our ability to achieve success if we busy ourselves with the unknown question of *how* we will finally realize our goal. *How* is none of our business. We are responsible for making clear to the universe *what* we want and then aligning our lives to prove we are sincere.

We do this by taking the steps necessary for success. This means we take the class, join the gym, check out the possibilities, ask the questions and make any required changes in our lives and consciousness. The exact *how* of how are we going to get from where we are to where we want to be is better left up to Spirit.

The old saying that God works in mysterious ways is true only because it is a mystery to us – not to God. The child who asks the parent to take them to the amusement park does not concern himself or herself with the parent obtaining the day off from work, arranging for younger siblings to have a sitter, saving the money for the admission charges and food, or how they will get to the park. That's all taken care of by the parent. We have a wise and loving parent in the form of God. Spirit can produce results and opportunities far beyond our imagination, *if* we are willing to allow God to work in our lives.

This does not mean that we are privy to each and every individual step along the way. At times we may question whether or not our success is as guaranteed as we originally thought it was. This was certainly the case with the late Rev. Dr. Robert H. Schuller. Dr. Schuller was the founding pastor of one of the most well-known churches in the world. His weekly show, *Hour of Power,* broadcast from what was then the Crystal Cathedral, was seen by hundreds of thousands of people on television. During the height of the ministry, Dr. Schuller had a large staff of ministers working with him to serve the congregation which worshiped at the church both in person and via satellite.

His life was not always this way. As a young minister, Dr. Schuller and his wife left the Midwest and journeyed across the country to a then-small community in Orange County, California. His ministry began preaching from the tarred roof of the snack bar in a drive-in theater. He was laughed at and ridiculed by other preachers. His goal was to make church accessible for everyone. People who could not afford fancy Sunday clothes showed up. Parents brought their children along to church with the wee ones still in their pajamas. Invalids who were too sick or too embarrassed to be wheeled into a building were driven to a place where they could worship and find hope.

Dr. Schuller's vision was assured of success because he knew it was possible. I have heard this same man speak on talk shows and write in his many books about times of doubt and uncertainty. He did not complain to God. He dropped to his knees, asked for direction, guidance and strength, and then got up and continued with his ministry. A bank would approve a loan, a parishioner would make a donation, or a zoning commissioner would change her mind. Spirit always provided.

Did Dr. Schuller always know exactly how things would work out for the highest good? According to him, that was frequently not the case. But his unshakable faith in the process allowed him the means to continue.

Our faith will be challenged. My friend, Marie, once told me it helps her to do some good old fashioned "knee praying" when times are rough. This is not an act of petitioning God or of begging God to bless her. It is a way of humbling herself and remembering that she is not powerless. She is reminding herself of her magnificence. She is taking the time to stop what she is doing, to call to mind that she, like all of us, is the perfect and unique manifestation of Spirit. She may not rise to her feet with the solution to the problem or an immediate answer to her question. But she does feel better afterward due to an increased awareness of divine right action being at work in her life.

How Strong Is Your Desire?

A strong, deeply rooted desire is the starting point of all achievement – we must remind ourselves of that from time-to-time. It is easy to get caught up in the daily chores and lose sight of the goal. We can become easily discouraged and even give up all together if we do not remind ourselves of the end result regularly. The practical side of practice is one way to do this. Here are several exercises and suggestions that can be incorporated in your practice as you continue to discover and live your.

Exercise #6 - Writing Lists

Create lists. Make a list of what you want, another list of what you do not want and a list of the things for which you are thankful, including your blessings or demonstrations.

What you want: Create a list of top goal items and the target dates by which you expect to manifest those goals. Rev. Edwene Gaines teaches a method working on twelve goals at a time. Twelve is significant because metaphysically it represents spiritual fulfillment and divine organization, e.g., twelve tribes of Israel or the twelve apostles. Some goals on my list are major ones; some are less significant in the overall scheme of my life, but no less important to me in seeing them as a reality. Decide on twelve goals for yourself that will move you in the direction of your vision and assign a target date for the completion of that goal.

Each morning review the list three times, visualize yourself experiencing each of the items, and prayerfully ask God what it is you have to change in order to achieve those goals. Then, repeat the same thing at night before you go to bed. Manifestation of your goals is not the challenge – you may realize many of your goals before your target dates or even before a goal reaches your current list, e.g., like my "private jet" manifestation that has never been on my "top twelve." The challenge for me is which item I shall next move from my master list to the top twelve!

What you don't want: Creating a list of what we *don't* want in our lives can be equally fulfilling and move us positively toward our goals. This particular exercise will cause you to admit what is not working in your life. It is easy to put up with situations, to settle for less than our true desires. Settling always creates resentment to some degree. That same resentment will make change even more difficult. Find out what you are no longer willing to tolerate in your life and make the necessary changes to move on. Some people are more interested in the "fluff" of spirituality ("pink cloud metaphysicians") and someone like that might run in horror from this exercise.

This type of individual is not interested in looking at *anything* that needs to be changed or that might be "wrong." They believe that if we dwell on the negative we are giving it power in our lives. This exercise is not about dwelling on what's wrong. *It is about acknowledging what needs to be changed in our consciousness so we can move forward in our mission.* A great way to physically remove these items from your life is to take the list and rip it up into a ceremonial burning bowl or fireplace. This ritual can have a tremendous impact on our consciousness as a tool to physically experience release.

Lists of gratitude: Emma Curtis Hopkins, one of the foremost people in the field of mental healing techniques, kept a "List of Evidentials," a list of the healings in which she had been privileged to participate. (Evidentials = Evidence of the healing power of prayer) This third list can be vital to our consistent success because it provides encouragement from our own experience at times when we may need a boost. A high school teacher I know has containers he calls his "Sunshine Boxes." He started out years ago with one and now has several. They are filled with cards and letters of appreciation he has received since he started teaching from students, parents and colleagues. They bring "sunshine" into his life on difficult days or through trying circumstance. Whatever you decided to use, be willing to keep track of all the good you experience. Our joys becoming overflowing as soon as we begin to look for things in our life for which to be thankful.

Exercise # 7 - Review

Reviewing our lists and other writings embeds into our conscious and subconscious mind the desires about which we have written. A review of previous writings then gives way to new writings, our feelings about past and current goals. It allows us the opportunity to re-examine our motives and make course corrections if necessary.

Exercise #8 - Meditate

There are a multitude of meditation practices available from which to choose. Taking time to still our chattering minds and listen to our deepest thoughts will center us, allowing us to focus on the moment. Extensive training in meditative practices can be enriching and literally a life's work all unto itself. But meditation does not have to be esoteric, nor does it require years of training to begin. Meditation can consist of gazing at a candle, closing our eyes and listening to our breathing or chanting. It can be taking a walk in the woods. It is the space we provide for Spirit to enter into our conscious recognition and guide us through intuition.

Early morning, *after* I've started the coffee pot, is my favorite time to meditate. I find waking up before sunrise is an especially peaceful and empowering gift I can give myself. In the warmer months I meditate outside in our gazebo, situated between the herb and shade gardens. The world is the quietest at this time. It can feel like you are the one setting the standard for the day – and perhaps we are!

I like setting the tone for my experiences. In my job as a flight attendant, I do this every time I board the aircraft, blessing the plane, the crew and all the passengers. I practice sitting and breathing. Sometimes I visualize being the mountain, or the tree, or the lake, but most of the time I just breathe. I use this time to check in with my body. Our bodies are infinitely wise and will tell us exactly what we need to know. By just asking our bodies what they need to express, we open our intuitive mind to guide us.

Practitioners of this method are frequently accused of just making up answers or imagining that their palpitating heart or sore knee is "talking" to them. I do not happen to believe that we are fooling ourselves, but what if we *are* making it up? How is that different than our lives in general? We are each individually and collectively "making it up," the "it" being our own lives and the global and local communities in which we live. Besides, it's fun!

Exercise # 9 - Journaling

Journaling is by far one of the most essential tools in our success. By keeping an accurate record of the events in our lives, our emotional responses and innermost feelings, we create a reference point for ourselves. We can chart where we have been, the progress we have made and the areas in which we might continue to improve. Rest assured that journaling is easy and fun! If you are one to use a pen you have many beautiful journals from which to choose at any number of bookstores.

For those of us more computer-oriented, journaling takes on an even more exciting aspect. Because we use both of our hands on the keyboard we are affectively utilizing both left and right brain functions. Another feature about journaling with a word processing program is the ability to review our writings for key words, phrases or situations using the "Find" or "Search" functions. I've been amazed when I've used this feature to discover particular words or phrases I've used repeatedly over the years.

I've had many clients and students tell me they simply cannot journal! To tell a writer you can't write is like telling him you can't breathe. Everyone can write, but quite a number of non-journalists are *afraid* to write. People are afraid someone will read what they write; but what if it is something wonderful to help others or save the world! Or they're afraid that it won't mean anything or move them in some way toward their goals.

Hogwash. If you feel you can't write, get a journal and pen, or run—not walk—to your computer and start writing about why you can't write. You might be pleasantly surprised, even shocked, to find out just what is in your fingers, just waiting for the chance to express itself! The way to write is *write*. No excuses, no reasons, no evading the issue. *Just write!* For more information on journaling and using writing as a tool for transformation, I once again recommend *The Artist's Way: A Spiritual Path to Higher Creativity*, by Julia Cameron with Mark Bryan (1992). It's been out for over twenty years, but the principles she presents are timeless for anyone who wants more clarity and creativity in their life.

Exercise # 10 - Ask, "Why?"

No worthwhile quest will crumble under questioning. If we are unable to state why we want to accomplish a goal we may find success to be illusive or delayed. The answer may be that we feel a strong desire. That, in and of itself, may be all the answer we need, or it could be a excuse for feeling victimized in our current situation and just wanting relief. By regularly questioning our desires and motives we open up to being further guided by Spirit, which may, in turn, open our eyes to hidden agendas or secret motives. We may discover that our desire for something material is only a weak physical representation of a more personal and inner desire for satisfaction. That fulfillment can appear only by changing our belief system about ourselves.

Exercise #11 - Daily Thought or Focus

A "Thought for the Day" can give us an additional boost in times of difficulty or an appropriately placed kick in the rear, if necessary. Wayne Dyer, Marianne Williamson, Deepak Chopra, Louise Hay and many other authors all have beautiful daily calendars for this purpose. Almost every household owns a Bible, still the number one all-time best seller ever published. Read the book of Proverbs in the Bible; it's full of gems to guide your life. (Note: Stay clear of the book of Lamentations. Save it for a day when you need a good cry and the movie *Beaches* is not available to you.)

Science of Mind® magazine and the *Daily Word* are monthly magazines that offer inspiring quotations and an affirmative prayer, meditation and uplifting reading material. My books *Meditations for Life!* and *Meditations for Life! – The Wisdom of Women* have been found helpful by many people for a centering thought. You can also open any inspirational book or magazine at random and the read the first page or section upon which your eyes fall. It is a perfect means of allowing Spirit to guide you intuitively to exactly what you need to know at that moment. I even used that method one time with *Popular Mechanics* – and it still worked!

Another method is to decide the focus for the day. For example, today might be about meditation, the next about cleaning and the following day about fun. We can determine a particular focus by reviewing our vision and mission statements daily. While those statements for our life will not normally change a great deal, the method of how we are carrying them out will be altered by our current circumstances.

When I am privileged to officiate at weddings I remind the couple that as the years go by their marriage will change. It's unreasonable to think that we can change as individuals without that having an effect on our relationships. But in successful, long-term relationships what doesn't change is the loving, trusting foundation upon which the marriage is based. The same is true of our vision and mission statements. While it would be counterproductive to change them frequently, slight changes and tweaks will probably occur for you as you continue toward the bliss your vision seeks to create.

Exercise #12 - Forgive - <u>DAILY!</u>

Lack of forgiveness will stop or delay our progress. It will also affect us in other ways. Holding grudges, or refusing to forgive others and ourselves, will eventually cause us harm by manifesting as physical and psychological illnesses.

As you are closing your eyes at night, forgive and release yourself and all others of any resentment, anger or disappointment. Start with yourself; many people are so busy blaming others they fail to recognize their own responsibility for the situations in which they find themselves. If we can't forgive ourselves, trying to forgive others will become frustrating for us. After we review our own activities, move out to others in your immediate life that come to mind, then on to social or racial groups and nations. Remember throughout the day to release yourself from guilt and harsh judgments. Refuse to judge others, regardless of the circumstances.

I would be lying if I told you I did this only once for each person with whom I had a gripe. The first time I used this method I thought I'd never stop running out of people to forgive, or people who I wanted to forgive me! Sometimes the face or name of a person just comes into my consciousness. At that moment there may be nothing in particular for which I feel I need to forgive them. But, my rule is this: If someone's face or name pops into my head, they get included. It's not up to me to decide why these things occur. It is my choice to act upon spiritual intuition and divine guidance. At times in my life I've had so much to forgive about myself that I've fallen asleep long before I got to anyone else.

This is an exercise we must continue throughout our lifetime. Part of being human means we make mistakes. We cannot take chances and risks without the possibility that our actions may not work out the way we originally planned. If we are not willing to make mistakes then we will not even start a project, or will give up at the first sign of difficulty. Forgiving ourselves for these mistakes is essential. Missing the mark is not a huge issue, unless we choose to make it so or refuse to let it go. Forgiveness of others and ourselves opens us to releasing the past, enjoying the present and moving powerfully into the future.

Forgiveness is probably the most powerful act you can perform to live a life of bliss. The persons we want most *not* to forgive are the ones who most need our forgiveness. Start with them and continue with the exercise until you feel a sense of relief or peace. You will not regret it, but you will be surprised at the blessings that are waiting in the wings to be showered down upon you.

I have just one last thought about forgiveness, just in case you have something in your life to which this applies. People often ask me how to forgive someone or something that they feel is unforgiveable. Inevitably these situations fall into two categories: abuse (of various types) and mass murder. I personally believe everyone and everything deserves forgiveness; whether or not you agree with that is for you to decide. But, if you feel someone in your past doesn't deserve to be forgiven, consider this: While they may or may not deserve your forgiveness, you do.

Grudges and resentment maintain a psychic link to the persons involved or to the event. The more tenaciously we refuse to forgive the stronger that link becomes. And, in the process, we find our own lives falling apart through failed relationships, health issues or financial difficulties. In most cases, the perpetrator of such horrible acts has long since passed on or couldn't care less about what has happened. That leaves only us to decide how much energy we want to place on the situation.

Additionally, something almost magical happens when we finally decide to forgive a long-held grievance. In many cases soon after we let go of the anger, pain and sorrow, the other person experiences a release as well. Families have been reunited, debts repaid and fences mended just because one person involved decided to forgive. Isn't that at least worth a try? If you're still not convinced, consider another quote I like to use to remind myself to let go of the past:

You've suffered long enough. Are you willing to try something else?

Exercise #13 - Goal target date

Review your top twelve goals and the target date. Are the targets realistic, believable? Does it make you nervous or excited? Write about those feelings in your journal and meditate on them. If you are approaching a target date, are you certain you will accomplish the goal on or before that date? Have circumstances changed so that the date needs to be adjusted forward or backward in time? It's okay to do that.

It's also perfectly acceptable and expected that you may look over your list and realize you no longer desire a goal. Placing it on the list will clarify your true desires. If you no longer wish for an item or circumstance, thank Spirit and remove it. The space will then be occupied by a new goal more in line with your current thinking.

Exercise #14 - Giving Thanks and Showing Appreciation

While retiring for the night is a great time for forgiving, waking up in the morning provides a unique opportunity to give thanks. I like to do "cat stretches" in the morning, instead of leaping out of bed. It helps to move our bodies from a night of lying there to a day of upright movement. As I do that and before getting out of bed I give thanks for anything in my life for which I am thankful. Imagine starting your day with heartfelt appreciation instead of dread about the world situation at that moment or all the chores you may have chosen to plan for that day.

Acknowledging our appreciation makes space for even more good in our lives. We thank Spirit for the wondrous universe in which we live. We give thanks by showing our appreciation for our own willingness to grow and change. We can thank others for the kindness we are shown throughout the day. In turn, the kindness we show to others is our way of giving thanks for the unity of all life.

Become aware of the global community and the important part you play in it. Being part of the human race, inhabiting an interdependent ecosystem, makes us part of a larger community than most people realize. This global community is of the utmost importance. It is the foundation of all the other communities in which we reside, our local community, our communities based on lifestyle, sexual orientation, race, or political affiliation and the core community we call family.

As such, we can give additional thanks by supporting the global community, by being aware of the impact our actions have on the planet. Using green products, recycling and conserving resources are just some of the obvious ways we can help the environment. Other less obvious ways are the consideration we can show for people we meet on the street, while driving or in long lines at stores. We can bless others as we go through our day by our kindness, helpful attitude and sincere desires to serve.

Exercise #15 - Release

Let go and let God. This phrase sounds far too simplistic for many in-charge types of people. It is also the perfect way of getting off our manipulation of life and back to the blissful workings of Spirit. This may sound a little airy-fairy, the "go with the flow attitude," but it is not without direction. We can let go and let God because we have already set the course, input the desire and started the ball rolling. We can go with the flow because we have carefully chosen the river or the stream in which to swim. One person told me he almost always got a good night's sleep by praying, "God, I worked the day shift. Now it's your turn." We could all learn to form a better partnership with Divine Wisdom. Releasing our desires is an excellent way to begin. While waiting impatiently for an elevator one day my eyes glanced at a sign in the shop next to where I was standing. It read:

Good Morning! This is God.
I'm going to handle all your problems today.
Won't be needing your help.
Enjoy yourself
and have a nice day!

Exercise #16 - Have Fun!

This is not all about working! If you are extremely structured and analytical you may need to schedule time to play. You may have to force yourself to have fun. Do it! Enlist the aid of friends who know how to play. I learned how from children I observed. At one time I had a "play alarm" of sorts. I used to have two cats, both with individual personalities. When one of them thought I had been at the computer long enough he would come to my desk and place both paws on the keyboard or flop their head against my leg. It was his way of saying it was time to go into the living room for a kitty massage, his daily brushing or a wrestling session. If I refused to go, I found a cat on the desk, laying on my arm or my computer mouse. He was both relentless, so I learned not to avoid this form of play in my life.

At first all these new and detailed activities may seem to leave you little time for play, let alone having the time to see the unfolding of your vision. You do not want to lose sight of why you are doing this all in the first place: To live your bliss. If these exercises become too much of a chore you may feel too busy getting ready to live your bliss to actually live your bliss! Pick one or a few things at first. Be aware of the changes in your life and you will desire to add more. With time, each step will take less and less time.

As we stop judging others and start blessing them, we have fewer things about which to complain. Our joys and blessings multiply. Our daily attitude is one of awe, joy and bliss. Practice does not make perfect. The practice is the perfection. The practice shows us how we can improve, how well we are doing and just how far we have come up until now. To achieve the bliss we desire and continue that ongoing lifestyle there is one more factor to consider. That factor is *Purpose.*

Chapter Six

Purpose

The last of the five "P's" is Purpose. This step is the underlying necessity behind the previous four steps. Our purpose is that which propels us into the action. It is what permits us to accomplish the goals on our path. In discussing purpose as the fifth step in creating a life worth living, it becomes a reminder of our very reasons for our desires.

Forgetting Our Purpose

It is easy to get into doing "it," whatever "it" is, and forget our purpose. There is a logical reason for this and especially true for people with an inclination to being obsessed with accomplishing goals. Our purpose holds a dual role. Part of its function is to act in a capacity much like a supervisor. It stands quietly in the background overseeing all the activity in our lives. At the same time it is the real reason there is activity in the first place. It is the basis for our activities. It is also synonymous with our vision.

It is crucial to our success for us to regularly remember our purpose in any activity. This is why our vision statement is so important. A vision statement gives structure to our core desires. It provides the matrix by which we can then build a life worth living. Whenever we have decisions to make we can recall our vision statement and ask, "Does doing or not doing what it is I am contemplating at this moment align with or detract from my vision?"

Fulfilling our vision leads to a more blissful life. At the same time we have other smaller purposes that assist in accomplishing goals leading us along our path. Dreaming, meditating, visioning and visualizing are examples of activities resulting in the alignment of our lives, thereby moving closer to achieving our bliss.

We can also inquire of our intention by engaging in various conflicting activities or in the goals we set for ourselves. This allows us to clarify our vision. It guarantees that the time we spend in activities is truly productive and not just spending time being busy.

Doing It For Ourselves

One way we can accomplish this is to do whatever it is we are doing for the purpose of pleasing ourselves. Does this sound selfish? It is not. I'm not suggesting that we give up our responsibilities, do only for ourselves or stop loving other people. Keeping clear about our vision means in part that it must be something we can personally commit to doing. If we do not enjoy what we are doing it is unlikely we will be very happy. It is also highly doubtful we will succeed in fulfilling our commitments to others or ourselves.

Obligations to other people, to family, to friends, to society in general and to so many other persons, places and things inside and outside of their own lives cause a tremendous amount of stress for many people. Perhaps you can relate to this when certain holidays roll around. People can find themselves in exactly the position about which Ashleigh Brilliant wrote when I was in high school. He said that the definition of prosperity in America was buying things we don't really want, with money we don't have, to impress people we don't like. It's a mouthful, but I believe there's more than a grain of truth in his statement. If we really are not "in the spirit" holiday cards become an expensive burden instead of the messengers of joy and love for which they are intended.

I stopped sending Christmas and Hanukkah cards many years ago to people I see frequently. I send very few if any cards to friends locally. Even my list for people far away has become shorter and shorter. Part of this is due to my daily use of social media, email and texting to stay in touch with people in my city and around the world on a more frequent basis than I did before the Internet.

The other part is my belief in the purpose of my vision. Anything, or any*one*, which does not support my vision, has no place in my life. At least twice a year I clean out my contact and mailing lists. The following exercise will free you in ways you cannot even imagine. It will also push some major buttons, but we all need that from time-to-time, me included.

Exercise #17 – Contact List Housecleaning

Start with the contact list in the email program you use most. This may be a week-long project if you have several email accounts, so take it one step at a time. Set aside 15 or 20 minutes and then stop so it doesn't become overwhelming.

If you can title your list you might use something like, "By Invitation Only." If that's not possible then keep a mental attitude that you are including only information for people who support you and your vision. (This is the button-pushing part.)

Continue this process *at least* once a year. I do it twice a year – once during my birthday month (May) and once before the end of the earth's annual cycle (October 31). For me it's a great way to begin my next birthday year or the next 12-month earth cycle, fresh and new!

It's not an easy task and you may discover more than a quandary or two in the process. You will find some people you *wish* would support you and your vision, but they do not. Why are they in your life? Some might be there for the glorious purpose of reflecting your own self-doubts. If some people are on another path then let them go their own way. Sometimes they may need to leave us, or we need to leave them, for a period of time. It may only be weeks or months. It might be years. It might be for the rest of this lifetime. Life is eternal and you *will* re-enter each other's lives if and when you need to do so.

There may be family or business associates with whom you do not spend a great deal, if any, personal time. Again, if having them in your life serves a purpose for the fulfillment of your vision, retain them. If someone is not contributing to your happiness then there are questions you must ask yourself that you alone can answer.

The same non-attachment we must practice with our possessions must be practiced with people. It does not mean we do not love them. It means we love them enough to allow them to chart their own course. It means we love ourselves enough to live our vision. People in our lives may very well have the potential to support us or be supported by us.

Just remember,

You cannot have a relationship with someone's potential.

God knows I have tried that many times in my life and I'm here to tell you it wasn't pretty! It's much like trying to teach a pig to sing. It wastes your time and it annoys the pig.

Letting Go

Just as certain people may no longer belong in our lives today, certain activities may have also outlived their appropriateness. At the same time, other people and activities may not be exactly in line with our vision but we will continue to have them in our lives. For example, few of us are going to discard our blood relatives simply because their lifestyles are diametrically opposed to ours, though we might choose to spend the holidays with our family of choice rather than our family of birth. Likewise, we may continue to work in a job or career that is certainly not how we envision living our bliss. Why? Because through that job comes the financial means to support us while we are preparing to do what we desire to do.

I cannot tell you I *enjoyed* working full-time as a temporary legal secretary while I was also creating my first church. My idea was to work only as the pastor of a church and be paid well for my services to others. It did not work out that way. I did not have the consciousness at the time to produce the desired result. I could have chosen to complain about that, to make my fledgling congregation wrong and go into the legal department everyday with a scowl on my face because I was in front of a computer instead of behind a pulpit.

I ministered wherever I was. I rejoiced in the financial support I was receiving as a legal secretary. I was open to the blessings that the temp job offered me. Though I was employed full-time, my expertise in that position allowed me more free time than the employee I was replacing. My superiors allowed me to use that extra time to write the newsletter for my ministry, work on my Sunday talks, make phone calls and utilize the office laser printer and copy machine for church bulletins and newsletters.

My willingness to "serve where planted" opened unexpected opportunities for me. The expertise I possessed in areas outside my job assignment was utilized. I became the interdepartmental liaison for a new computer system. I was one of the few people who knew how to deal with the glitches in the new system. I could take an outside and unattached viewpoint when department heads seemed to be at odds with one another in the implementation of the new procedures.

Another time I was called upon to act as a mediator at a non-profit organization for which one of the attorneys volunteered. All this was a terrific lesson for me in recognizing that Spirit can lead us in our vision quest to experiences which will enrich us and help others, too…*if* we will get out of Spirit's way and allow It to do Its work!

All these blessings occurred because I kept my vision at the forefront of my life. I never apologized for needing time away from my temporary position to visit a sick church member or perform a memorial service during the workweek. I never apologized to my congregation that I did not have a fancy church building with a lavish counseling office or that they had a pastor who worked downtown during the week as a secretary. I endured the scorn of other local ministers who laughed at my little church. I got through the pain of hearing rumors of disapproval from other ministers in my own domination because I was not doing church the way they were. None of this could have been possible if I had not kept my vision in mind at all times.

"Simple" does not always mean "Easy."

It was not always easy. Sometimes it was actually very difficult. It was all worth it. Why? Because today I can look back and see how far I have come to living a life of fulfillment and contentment. I wake up happy to be alive. I enjoy my life and my work. I have a ministry that reflects who I am: playful, loving, eclectic and just a little twisted! Not everyone who meets me is willing to make use of my services. I do not fit their pictures of a minister or counselor. That is fine with me. Without their belief that they could have a healing or make a change I couldn't do anything to assist them anyway.

The joy of life is that there are plenty of other ministers and counselors out there in the world that will fit their picture perfectly. I can easily bless them as they go on their way to find those people, usually shaking their heads at my lifestyle and me. Some people bless us by coming. Some people bless us by leaving. Help the people who come into your life. Release the ones who must go elsewhere. Love them all.

Your vision is a precious entity to which you are giving life. Recognize that. Nurture it as you would a new plant or any new life. Bring purpose to your purpose. This is done easily by envisioning your vision. Be willing to take time each day to *feel* what living your bliss would feel like.

Make lists of goals

Create those goal lists chronologically: daily goals; one-, three- and six-month goals; one-, three-, five- and ten-year plans

Visualize specific goals as being already accomplished

Dare to dream

Give life to those hopes, dreams and goals

Does this seem like a lot of work? It should. It is. No one said being successful was easy. Simple? Yes. Easy? It probably is not for most of us. The simple part is that we must be persistent in our efforts for success. Persistence in sticking to our purpose for living is vital to success. The amount of work required is not a burden since we are doing what we want to do in the pursuit or expression of our happiness.

Selfishness

There is a negative concept of selfishness about doing anything solely for ourselves. We must get past this if we are going to stay on purpose with our vision. Haven't you known people who believe whenever they do *anything* for themselves it is selfish and therefore bad? Doing for ourselves is not necessarily selfish, nor is being selfish, at times, a bad thing.

This can conflict with much of our upbringing: "Don't be so selfish! Take the smaller piece of cake!" "Why are you so selfish? Don't you think I deserve to rest too?" So the little girl grows up and always takes the smaller piece of cake, the less lucrative position, or the more economical car. The little boy grows up working very hard, stressing himself out over the smallest details and seldom takes time off work to enjoy time with loved ones or the fruits of his labor.

This is also the reason why our vision must be something which is truly personal to our own life, not the desires of someone else. If our vision is one that supports someone else's vision or goals instead of giving the gift we have to give, then we will not experience the fulfillment for which we are searching. It will not include giving of *our* unique and special gift. Without that element in our daily life we cannot feel the satisfaction of accomplishment. We are denying the expression of our very reason for existing in this particular time. We are also depriving the rest of the world of who we are as we masquerade as someone we are not.

Nurturing the Vision

For us to be on purpose we must see clearly and write about our vision every day. We should talk about our vision, though not necessarily to other people. In Matthew 6:6, Jesus told his followers to pray in their private room, or "closet" as some translations render that passage, meaning in the privacy of their own thoughts. If we choose to share private, personal goals and dreams with others it had better be with like-minded people who will support us in those precious desires.

I made that mistake by publicly using a new last name at one point in my life. This special and sacred name was given to me in ritual space. It was not a good idea to make it public. Many people laughed at me during a time when I was making a huge life transition and in the midst of a grieving/healing process. I found myself engaged in conversations with people I hardly knew discussing intimate details with regard to these changes. It would have been kinder to myself to keep that information private, which is why I returned to using my birth name again in my work.

Staying on purpose with our vision creates results in our lives. The majority of people do not have a vision, nor are they willing to commit to the course of action which will change their lives for the better. They are the same people who will be quick to criticize our guaranteed success, as well as do their best to dash to pieces our hopes, dreams and goals. Be willing to make that mistake at least once. I can assure you it will be a growth experience. Do not make it again, at least not with the same person. To do so can harm you and your ability to express who you are.

Getting Support

Consistent persistence requires constant vigilance on our parts. It is important that we all have a strong support system. Friends and family can be there for us, as we can be for them. Support can be as simple as that knowing smile over a cup of coffee, or a hug that says it will all be okay sooner than we think, or when things are not going exactly the way we think they should. A therapist, coach or counselor coupled with a spiritual guide (mentor, prayer practitioner or minister) becomes a powerful aid in helping us remember who we are.

Sticking with the same people year after year develops the history that is so dynamic when times are rough. When I need to hear it, my prayer practitioner reminds me of where I *used* to be. It is empowering to have her remind me of the problems I have overcome in the past. She never allows me to see myself as anything less than magnificent, usually at a time when I am seeing myself somewhat differently.

Clarity of purpose and the desire to stay on purpose will allow happiness to blossom and grow in your life. A major step in clarifying our purpose is to understand our intention about any endeavor. What may appear to be our intention might be very different than the actual reason we end up doing something. The last chapter will assist you in establishing a *Clear Intention* in your life.

Chapter Seven

Clear Intention

Most people do not have a clue when it comes to true intention in life. A routine in life easily becomes a rut when day-after-day, year-after-year we stay in the same nowhere job that allows us to just get by. The workweek looks dismal at best for the 9-to-5 crowds. Monday is dreaded because we have to go back "there." We go about our duties with only 5pm on Friday as our goal. The weekend becomes a feeble attempt at recreation and pleasure. Excesses of what will result in hopelessness, depression and financial burden accompany the attempts to have fun. Sadly, when some are asked about their weekends, they reply, "I must have had a good time. I don't remember a thing!"

Change

Doing what we have always done or living life the way we think we should is not clear intention. It could be, if we were happy about that life, but most people are not. A great number of people do not like their jobs or careers. If this describes you, your life might reflect survival and resignation, but not intention. Unfortunately, this situation feels like a no-win, dead-end situation, with a total inability to see any change as possible.

Jesus gave us the keys to the kingdom of heaven. He did this by showing us through the miracles that it is done unto us as we believe. Ernest Holmes, the founder of the Science of Mind® philosophy and Religious Science movement, wrote that to change our lives we must change our thinking. The belief that Jesus demonstrated and the thinking about which Dr. Holmes taught are the very same thing. They are not what we *wish* would happen. They are not what we *hope* will happen. Our beliefs are the foundations by which we develop the basis for living, individually and as a people.

In-Tension

If we take apart the word *intention* we get: *in – tension*. Tension is something we have naturally, but are taught to avoid in everyday life. A certain amount of tension is required in life. If our muscles did not tense and flex we would be a blob of flesh and bones. The gravity that keeps us on the planet could be likened to a form of tension.

When we become clear in our intention in life we have our situation under control, much the same way we control a pet on a retractable leash. We let the leash out sometimes, allowing the pet to roam. At other times we reel the pet in to avoid a conflict or to protect the animal. If we let the pet off the leash we run the risk of it wandering off for a period of time, injuring it or even being killed. Because we accept the responsibility that comes with pet ownership, we protect our pets by keeping them on a leash or confining them to a small area. If we allow them to run free it is only when we are confident the area is safe for them. We must care just as much about whatever we are doing in the other parts of our daily lives.

Making Decisions

If we know what we want and believe in ourselves, making decisions is much simpler. Again, simple frequently does not mean easy. It is far easier to discuss what we do *not* want than what we *do* want. This is due to the fact that what we focus our attention on multiplies in our life. It becomes our intention. If we are low on cash we may begin concentrating on our financial lack. The more we think about what we do not have the more concerned about our situation we become. We forget about any possible solution and focus on the problem. We do not want to be penniless. But how much money will be enough? How soon do we need it? These questions become unanswerable because we have become so entangled in the problem that our lack chokes off all possible release.

Answering the questions means we must make a decision. Will our decision be the right one? Do we have the information we need to make an intelligent choice? We are taking responsibility. If things do not turn out the way we expect we will have only ourselves to blame! A familiar old character has just entered onto the stage in the play we call "Life." That character is *Fear*.

Enter: FEAR

We have already met Fear in chapter three. It is once again interfering (*enter* + *fearing*) with our ability to make a decision. It is time to throw fear out of our lives and build on the firm foundation that we have laid.

This does not mean we ignore difficult situations, refuse to count the costs or move forth blindly. By applying the Principles taught in this book and by working through the exercises presented, fear can be eliminated as a cause for failure or stagnation. It is not going to happen overnight for most of us. There are very few "overnight successes." When we are suddenly aware of a popular performer it may appear that he or she is an overnight success. We are not usually privy to the years of preparation, the lean times this person has had to endure, nor the sacrifices they have made. Regardless of the facts, they made something of themselves. We can too.

If we are spiritually and mentally alert, and our situation does not turn out the way we expect it to, do we then assign blame to ourselves? No. We take *responsibility*, not blame, for the outcome. The joy in this recognition is that the clearer we become about what we want to put into life and get out of life, the easier it is to have the life we want to live, a life of bliss and happiness. Along with this clarity comes, not blame for a life that is a hot mess, but credit for having a life worth living.

The Key to Clear Intention

If the power of clear intention is acting on our desire, then the key is faith. It is faith in ourselves and faith in a power greater than ourselves, even though we understand that it is a power of which we are a part of or an expression of in human form. Faith is that assurance we feel deep within our gut – no matter what the appearance may be – that our success is secure.

We must develop not faith *in* God/Goddess (or Spirit, or Higher Power), but more accurately the faith *of* that presence. No one who believes in a universal intelligence or absolute power would ever consider that It has problems or issues with making decisions. It has been said of Jesus of Nazareth that he was able to make use of the healing power of God because he expected to be able to do so. Jesus was not surprised when the blind saw, the lame walked or the dead rose from the tomb. He might have been surprised if his spoken word and prayers were *not* made manifest immediately, but he was never surprised at the outcome. He spoke his word and expected results. We must be that sure of the same power at our disposal.

That kind of confidence cannot come from outside sources. If we are constantly waiting for mom, dad or that special someone to shower us with approval at the turn of every corner then we are destined to remain perpetually stuck. Of course it is gratifying to receive the approval and support of others, but we can only expect to have our path clear if we believe in our decisions and ourselves.

Now what?

Discovering and living your bliss is an inside job, each of us individually and unique uncovering our gift for the planet. You already have all that it takes within you to succeed. By now you have most likely discovered what it is in life you want to, need to and must do. If not, perhaps you are not yet ready to accept your magnificence. If that is the case, be at peace with where you are. If you have discovered your bliss, then begin today to live it by committing to your vision and acting on your mission.

Take a deep breath – a *very* deep breath. If you have read and studied this book you have completed a course in changing your consciousness. That is no small feat. Just by reaching out to better yourself and your situations in life you have already begun the road to more happiness, prosperity and satisfaction.

There will be times that you may doubt yourself. If or when that time comes when you lack what you consider to be sufficient faith, would you be willing to borrow some of mine? It is my prayer treatment that you are experiencing a life-changing transformation that expressed a level of magnificence unknown to you up until now. Step out of your own way. Walk with confidence into a new life – a life truly worth living!

Appendix

Exercise - Creating the Vision

Take time for each of these questions as you begin to formulate your vision. Some of the questions are ones I've developed over the past two decades. A few are ones I have received from others over the years. I apologize in advance for not being able to give credit where credit is due to those people.

Go with your first thought, no matter how outrageous, no matter how selfish, no matter how "inappropriate." Do not rush through them. Journal about each of them, write about your joy, your anger, or whatever other emotion becomes apparent. Each of these questions is designed to more fully uncover what you may have been hiding from yourself and the planet.

What one talent, as yet undeveloped, would you be willing to explore?

What would you like to be your biggest triumph?

What would you study if you were given a scholarship to take care of all your personal and educational expenses?

What story have you carried around about how you "wish you would have…?"

What is the payoff for continuing to carry this story around?

What is your biggest piece of unfinished business?

What risks would you take that you haven't taken so far?

What major effort are you taking, or planning to take, which will make your vision a reality?

By what would you most like to be surprised?

What new major indulgence would you be willing to experience?

What is the biggest, best opportunity awaiting you?

What would you like most to change about yourself? Why?

If you were your best friend, what advice would you give yourself?

If you had three wishes (not involving money, health or world peace), what would they be? Why?

Finally, what questions do you still have? Spend time in mindful meditation and allow those answers to be revealed to you.

Suggested Reading

Do What You Love, and the Money Will Follow: Discovering Your Right Livelihood, by Marsha Sinetar. Copyright © 1987 by Dr. Marsha Sinetar. Published by Dell Publishing (Random House).

Doing What You Love—Loving What You Do, by Robert Anthony. Copyright © 1991 by Robert Anthony. Published by Berkley Trade.

Feel the Fear and Do It Anyway, by Dr. Susan Jeffers. Copyright © 1987 by Susan Jeffers. Published by Ballantine Books.

Gifts from Eykis, by Dr. Wayne Dyer. Copyright © 1983 by Wayne Dyer. Published by Simon and Schuster, Inc.

Meditations for Life!, by Terry Drew Karanen, (formerly *Treatments for Life!*, by Terry LoneWolf). Copyright © 1996 by Terry LoneWolf. Published by Support Services Unlimited.

Meditations for Life!—The Wisdom of Women, by Terry Drew Karanen. Copyright © 1997 by Terry Drew Karanen. Published by LoneWolf Publishing.

Open Your Mind to Prosperity, by Dr. Catherine Ponder, Copyright © 1971 by Unity School of Christianity. Copyright © transferred to Catherine Ponder August 1983. Published by DeVorss & Company.

Open Your Mind to Receive, by Dr. Catherine Ponder. Copyright © (date unknown) by Catherine Ponder (assumed). Publisher unknown.

Psycho-Cybernetics and Self-Fulfillment, by Dr. Maxwell Maltz. Copyright © 1970 by Maxwell Maltz. Published by Bantam Books.

Psycho-Cybernetics 2000 (a revitalization for the 21st Century of Dr. Maltz's original work), by Bobbe Sommer with Mark Falstein. Copyright © 1993 by Maxwell Maltz Psycho-Cybernetics Foundation, Inc. Published by Prentice Hall.

Real Magic, by Dr. Wayne W. Dyer. Copyright © 1992 by Wayne W. Dyer. Published by HarperCollins Publishers.

The Art of Being: 101 Ways to Practice Purpose in Your Life, by Dennis Merritt Jones. Copyright © 2004, 2008 by Dennis Merritt Jones. Published by Jeremy P. Tarcher/Penguin.

The Art of Uncertainty: How to Live in the Mystery of Life and Love It, by Dennis Merritt Jones. Copyright © 2011 by Dennis Merritt Jones. Published by Jeremy P. Tarcher/Penguin.

The Artist's Way, Julia Cameron with Mark Bryan. Copyright © 1992 by Julia Cameron. Published by G. P. Putnam's Sons.

The Dynamic Laws of Prosperity, by Dr. Catherine Ponder. Copyright © 1962 by Prentice-Hall, Inc. Published by Prentice-Hall, Inc.

The Four Spiritual Laws of Prosperity, by Edwene Gaines. Copyright © 2005 by Edwene Gaines. Published by Rodale, Inc.

The Life You Were Born to Live: A Guide to Finding Your Life Purpose, by Dan Millman. Copyright © 1993 by Dan Millman. Published by H. J. Kramer, Inc.

The Hebrew (Old) and Greek/Aramaic (New) Testaments of the Bible. Recommended translations for easy reading, understanding an accuracy are: *New World Translation of the Holy Scriptures* (WTBTS); *The Bible in Living English* (WTBTS); *The New English Bible with the Apocrypha* (Cambridge University Press); and, *The Living Bible* (Wheaton House Publishing).

The Power of Decision, by Raymond Charles Barker. Copyright © 1968, 1988 by Raymond Charles Barker. Published by Dodd, Mead & Company, Inc.

This Thing Called Life, by Ernest Holmes. Copyright © 1943 by Ernest Holmes. Published by G. P. Putnam's Sons.

This Thing Called You, by Ernest Holmes. Copyright © 1948 by Ernest Holmes. Published by G. P. Putnam's Sons.

Use The Cosmic 2x4 To Hit A Home Run: 5 Spiritual Steps to Overcome Adversity, by Judy Mattivi Morley, PhD. Copyright © 2013 by Judy Mattivi Morley, PhD. Published by Park Point Press.

Your (Re)Defining Moments: Becoming Who You Were Born to Be, by Dennis Merritt Jones. Copyright © 2013. Published by Jeremy P. Tarcher/Penguin.

What's My Type?: Use the Enneagram System of Nine Personality Types to Discover Your Best Self, by Kathleen V. Hurley and Theodore E. Dobson. Copyright © 1991 by Enneagram Resources, Inc. and Copyright © 1990 by Kathleen Hurley and Theodore Dobson. Published by HarperCollins Publishers.

Where Regret Cannot Find Me: Essays from the Spiritual Path, by David Ault. Copyright © 2013. Published by Xlibris.

Appreciation

There are numerous people to whom I'm genuinely grateful for being part of the creation and completion of this book. The following individuals have been kind enough to take their time, free of charge, to review, edit, critique, and (in some cases) argue with me! I am unable to fully express how much I appreciate the work, love and encouragement of David Ault, Arleen Bump, Jane Claypool, Marie Dolce, Paul Foltz, Bob Gale, Susan Granger, Maxine Kaye, Marilyn Leo, Debbie Maitland-Roland, James Mapes, Dennis Merritt Jones, Jaine Ryder, Edward Vilijoen and Kevin Wagner.

Michele Sevacko must be acknowledged separately. Not only has she given me sound advice over the years, but it was she who first decided I needed to write this book. Thanks, Chele!

I would be remiss if I didn't acknowledge my teachers and mentors over the past three decades as they have impacted the man I have become: Candice Beckett, Arleen Bump, Jane Claypool, Tom Costa, Michael Davidson, Ellen Debenport, Marie Dolce, Juanita Dunn, Edwene Gaines, Bob Gale, Zan Gaudioso, Jacob Glass, Christine Jeffers, Dennis Merritt Jones, Maxine Kaye, Cindy Sternberg Key, Marilyn Leo, Marilyn Miller, Charel Morris, Joe Paiva, Vetura Papke, Domenic Polifrone, Mary Ruth Huffer, Jaine Ryder, Sandhi Scott, Ron Scott, Carol Sheffield, J. Kennedy Shultz, Nancy Stepp, Helen Street, Jaye Taylor and Frank Vavrovsky.

To my fellow ministerial school student and spiritual counselor, Maureen Hoyt; and, my prayer partner, C.C. Coltrain, thank you for knowing the Truth about me when I've forgotten.

My mother, Timi Ruiz, continues to love and encourage me in ways beyond my comprehension. Somehow in spite of our differing religious views she continues to support me, honors my path and is proud of whom I've become. My sister, Tempest Miller, is always there when I *really* need her and not just when I *think* I need her.

Finally, to my partners, Paul Foltz and Kevin Wagner: How you put up with my crazy schedules, my multiple careers, my spiritual beliefs, my 98 shades of gray between the one percent of black and white in my thinking, and my inability to tell a story without a circuitous journey through more details than are necessary…thank you. I love you both and love the family we've created.

About the Author

Terry Drew Karanen began his professional service to others in 1985. His ministerial training was completed at both Ernest Holmes College (now Holmes Institute) through United Church of Religious Science at United Spirit Church in West Hollywood, California, and through Religious Science International at the First Church of Religious Science, Glendale, California. (Both organizations now make up Centers for Spiritual Living, Golden, Colorado.) He was ordained as a minister in 1996 at the Healing Light Center in Turtle Creek, Pennsylvania, by the late Rev. Kasandra Sutton. In 1998 the American Institute of Holistic Theology, Youngstown, Ohio, granted him a doctor of divinity degree. In 2011 he earned his master of social work degree from Temple University, Harrisburg, Pennsylvania, and holds a license as a social worker in the Commonwealth of Pennsylvania. His undergraduate degree is in social sciences from Thomas Edison State College, Trenton, New Jersey. He is currently affiliated as an ordained minster with Centers for Spiritual Living.

Terry has worked as a speaker, seminar facilitator and seminar coordinator throughout the United States, and assisted organizations with conflict resolution and collective focus through the creation of group vision and mission statements. In addition to founding and leading two Centers of Spiritual Living in Pennsylvania he has also served as spiritual leader for a Unity church. Two of his eight books have been used by major organizations in the training of their ministerial students.

Terry now serves others through his own company, *Terry Drew Karanen Ministries, LLC dba TDKM, LLC*. Additionally, he operates the non-profit *Spirit, Mind and Body Foundation*, a Focus Ministry of Centers for Spiritual Living. The Foundation seeks to integrate spiritual practices with healthy mental and physical living. 30 percent of the Foundation's gross income is granted quarterly through the *Frank Anthony Vavrovsky, Jr. Memorial Fund* in the form of an "Appreciation Award" to another organization or individual doing like-minded work for planetary peace.

Terry Drew Karanen

Terry makes his home in south central Pennsylvania on a two-acre property he shares with his two partners and their cats, as well as numerous other wild critters. He continues working as a career flight attendant for American Airlines.

For more information on Terry's work or to schedule him to speak for your organization refer to his website at: http://terrydrewkaranen.com or email him at: terry@terrydrewkaranen.com

Terry's weekly blog, "Making Sense of Life" and his essays can be found at: http://blog.terrydrewkaranen.com

Information on the work of Terry's Foundation can be found at: http://spiritmindbodyfoundation.org

"Making Sense of Life" – Daily version (Daily encouragements and spiritual practices) are published at: http://facebook.com/spiritmindbodyfoundation

Follow Terry on Twitter: @TerryDKaranen

Printed in the United States
By Bookmasters